An AMISH
CINDERELLA

T0268804

SHELLEY SHEPARD GRAY

An AMISH CINDERELLA

ZEBRA BOOKS
Kensington Publishing Corp.
kensingtonbooks.com

ZEBRA BOOKS are published by

Kensington Publishing Corp.
900 Third Avenue
New York, NY 10022

All Kensington titles, imprints, and distributed lines are available at special quantity discounts for bulk purchases for sales promotion, premiums,
fund-raising, and educational or institutional use.

Special book excerpts or customized printings can also be created to fit
specific needs. For details, write or phone the office of the Kensington
Sales Manager: Kensington Publishing Corp., 900 Third Avenue, New
York, NY 10022. Attn. Sales Department. Phone: 1-800-221-2647.

ZEBRA BOOKS and the Zebra logo Reg. U.S. Pat. & TM Off.

First Kensington Books hardcover and trade paperback printings:
October 2023
First Zebra Books mass market paperback printing: February 2025

ISBN-13: 978-1-4201-5549-5
ISBN-13: 978-1-4967-3990-2 (eBook)

10 9 8 7 6 5 4 3 2 1

Printed in the United States of America

"He will teach us His ways so we will walk in His paths."
Isaiah 2:3

Seeing ourselves as others see us wouldn't do much good—we wouldn't believe it anyway.
Amish proverb

Chapter 1

December
Apple Creek, Ohio

At last, it was December. Though Heart Beachy loved Christmas and all the festivities and traditions surrounding the birth of Jesus, she didn't care for the month all that much. As far as she was concerned, December was usually too busy, too filled with overblown expectations for the big day, and too cold.

Gazing at the clouds outside the kitchen window, at the way the gray skies seemed to cast a dull pall over the dormant plants and shrubs in the nearby flower beds, she almost . . . almost wished it was January.

At least in January the ground was usually covered in a thick blanket of snow. The fluffy white powder looked clean and bright. Plus, the frigid January temperatures encouraged folks to stay inside and relax. She would dearly love a day or two to relax.

Unfortunately, since it was forty-three degrees and there wasn't a patch of snow in sight, today would be a different story.

She turned away from the dreary landscape. Grabbing a dishcloth, she began wiping down the counters and tried to think of brighter things. Soon everyone in Apple Creek would be looking forward to building snowmen, gathering for Advent, and displaying Christmas cards. Neighbors would be wrapping presents and baking cookies.

Just like in years past.

Or, for those blessed to be in love, perhaps they'd go on a sleigh ride, complete with bells and ribbons on the sleigh and a prancing horse. Couples could glide down the lane, snug in warm blankets . . . or in each other's arms. It would be perfect.

Heart Beachy pressed a hand to the glass pane and dreamed about doing such things. If she had an outing planned with a handsome suitor, she'd make a new dress for it. Perhaps a cozy wool dress in a deep shade of cranberry. Her mother used to say that shades of red complemented Heart's blue eyes and blond hair nicely.

"*Nee*, Mamm didn't say that," Heart murmured out loud. What she actually said was, "Hazel, I do like you in red. It sets off your *beautiful* blue eyes."

Remembering how much she'd love to hear her mother's sweet words, Heart smiled. Her mother always had encouraging words of praise for her only child.

On the heels of that good memory was a far less ap-

pealing one. It never failed to make her cringe, but
Heart forced herself to remember it as well. Because
instead of hugging her *mamm* for making her feel special and good, all she'd ever done was scowl and state
that she hated her name and wanted to be called
"Heart" instead.

Though her words had been true—after all, who
really wanted to be named Hazel?—Heart wished she'd
held her tongue. Ack, but she'd been such a spoiled
child. Such a willful little girl. It was no wonder that at
least two afternoons a week Mamm would send Heart
out to go "help" her *daed* in his blacksmith workshop.

The barn had been hot and filled with dangerous
things, but her father had never seemed to mind her
being with him. He'd given her a little chair in the corner and small tasks to do.

Looking around the kitchen that was exactly the
way her mother had originally organized it twenty-five
years ago, she felt the same sense of loss she always
did around this time of year.

Her mother had died on November 30, four years
ago. Mamm, so sweet and pretty and bright, had died
just weeks after contracting the flu. No doctor could
give a reason why her mother hadn't survived. . . . She
just hadn't.

All Heart knew was that Katie Beachy's passing had
left a hole in the house that neither her husband nor her
daughter had been able to fill.

Not that either of them had ever tried.

Heart knew that if she had just one more day with
her mother, she'd be so happy. She'd tell her just how

much she loved her. How grateful she was to have such a sweet and loving *mamm*.

But, of course, wishes and dreams were for other folks. It seemed that so much of what she'd asked for never was going to come true. Maybe the Lord had decided that she already had enough for any young woman.

Before her dark thoughts descended deeper, the back door just off the kitchen opened with a rough *clack*.

"Heart, you have dinner on the table yet?" Daed called out as he bypassed the stationary tub next to the door and tromped into the kitchen.

She felt like pointing to the kitchen clock above the door. She served her father's midday meal at eleven o'clock sharp every day. Always. Her father had come in too early. "Not yet. I'll have it out soon."

"When?"

She rolled her eyes. "In seven minutes, Daed. When it's eleven."

He scowled. "It ain't ready early?"

"Nope."

"Heart." Her father had a deep, almost scratchy voice. That voice, combined with the fact that he was over six feet tall and a very muscular 250 pounds, made him an imposing presence.

She'd seen some men almost cower when he asked them a direct question. Actually, most people tended to give him a wide berth. He might be a very good blacksmith and a rather famous welder, but he wasn't much for company.

She, on the other hand, was well used to the way he barked questions and glowered at his surroundings. He wasn't a mean man. Not at all. It was more like the Lord had given him so many gifts working with hot metals that He hadn't seen the need to give Levi Beachy too many softer qualities.

She, like her mother, was well used to his bark.

"No sense in complaining, Daed. Your midday meal will be ready when it's ready. And that will be at eleven." When he started to complain, she added a bit cheekily, "Hold your horses."

His eyebrows snapped together, but he didn't erupt. Instead, he simply exhaled. "Fine. I'm gonna wash up."

"Danke." He turned and walked down the hall to the bathroom.

He always made that walk, even though the stationary tub was right next to the back door, and it contained his favorite scrubbing soap and fluffy hand towels. And there was a sink in the kitchen, too.

Nope, he always insisted on making that trek, all while keeping on his dirty boots. No matter how many times she'd asked him to remove them, he didn't listen. Not even when she explained how dirty they got her freshly swept floor. Or how stained his hands made the pristine guest bathroom sink.

He'd always look mystified about why a messy floor should concern him.

Knowing that some things would never change, she pulled out two bowls and silverware. Then decided to switch things up a bit. Maybe for once she'd wait to eat until later. Maybe after she went for a walk or something.

Carefully she spooned a hearty portion of shepherd's pie into his bowl. Ground beef mixed with fresh vegetables and thick gravy. The top layer of mashed potatoes was golden brown.

She'd just placed his dish on the table when her father returned.

His eyes lit up and he took his chair. "Ah, Heart. You do have a way with meat and potatoes."

This was high praise from her father, but as compliments went, it left a lot to be desired. "*Danke,* Daed."

After placing his napkin in his lap—Mamm had trained her father well in the basics of table manners—he looked at the empty space in front of her. "Where is your food?"

"I decided to wait to eat."

A line formed between his brows. "Why?"

"I'm not too hungry. Besides, the temperature isn't too cold today. I was thinking that I might go on a walk."

"Good thinking. It's nice to get out of the house."

After her father bowed his head in silent prayer, he dug in.

Heart sipped her water and mentally planned out the rest of her day. Most of the supper preparations were done, so after she returned from her walk, she could relax in the living room and maybe even work on a sewing project. Or begin work on her father's Christmas cards. He sent each of his clients a card. Well, she did. There were almost two hundred of those to address.

Several minutes passed before he spoke again. "Where are you going to walk to?"

"I'm not sure."

His gaze settled on hers. "You planning on visiting some of the neighbors?"

"Maybe." She hadn't really planned to visit anyone, but it was an idea.

"Mary Miller ain't far. Maybe you could check on her. She's got puppies, I heard."

Heart enjoyed Mary's company. She was easy to be around and usually in a good mood. Puppies were an added bonus. "I hadn't heard about the pups. I'll definitely have to go see them. Did her golden have the litter?"

He nodded. His blue eyes—the one thing she'd inherited from him—brightened. "I don't know anyone whose day wouldn't be made better by visiting a mess of golden retriever pups."

She smiled back at him. "You are right about that."

"Since you've been thinking about getting some work pet-sitting, you ought to stop by and see them. Maybe offer to give Mary a hand." He took another bite. "If you have time, that is."

Mary Miller's husband had passed away when Heart was just a child. To everyone's surprise, she'd never remarried. Instead, she seemed to enjoy her job, which was helping to care for elderly and ailing folks around the area. She usually brought her golden retriever with her and stayed in homes for weeks until her patient recovered or passed on to Heaven.

She'd helped Heart's *mamm* years ago as well. Knowing her father had a soft spot for Mary, Heart nodded. "I can make time to help Mary. *Danke* for the idea, Daed."

"It was nothing. Just be home by three o'clock."

"Why?"

"Someone's coming over who I want you to meet."

This conversation was getting curiouser and curiouser. Her father did blacksmithing and ironworks for lots of people, but none of them were of much interest to Heart. Actually, Daed seemed to prefer that his customers stay away from her. "Who's coming over?" she asked.

Her father looked almost smug. "You'll see. Just be home by three." Looking around the kitchen, he added, "And maybe you could make some of your monster cookies?"

He sounded so hopeful, she hid a smile. Her father might be several inches over six feet and built like a linebacker on a football team, but he had a soft spot for her special oversized cookies. He had no idea that making them took no time at all.

"*Jah,* Daed. I'll be happy to make those."

"*Gut.*" He scooted back his chair and strode to the door. It slammed behind him. Leaving behind a trail of dirt.

The right thing to do would be to eat her meal, sweep the floor, make the cookies, and wash the dishes. But she needed a break and wanted to enjoy at least an hour outside before she returned to all her chores.

Pleased with her decision, Heart covered the pie with some waxed paper, set it in the fridge, and walked out the door. She might be a twenty-five-year-old spinster, but she wasn't without a backbone.

Chapter 2

"Heart! What a nice surprise," Mary Miller exclaimed when she opened her door. "What brings you here today?"

"My father mentioned that you had a litter of new puppies. I wondered if I could see them?"

Mary's face turned into a wreath of smiles. "Yes, indeed. They're tiny now and still have their eyes closed, but Virginia knows you," she added over her shoulder as she led the way to the living room. "She won't mind you visiting."

"How many pups did she have?"

"Five!" Mary's dark brown eyes fairly glowed with happiness.

"Five puppies! That's wonderful-*gut.*"

"Virginia is tired, but pleased, I think."

Crouching down to the large wooden box with a blanket for Virginia and shredded paper for the pups, Heart gasped. As puppies were wont to do, they were piled all on top of each other and fast asleep. "Oh, Mary. They are adorable."

"Indeed they are. A litter of puppies is surely one of God's sweetest blessings." Reaching down, Mary gently rubbed the mother dog's head. "You did a good job, Virginia. It's a family to be proud of."

The hund thumped her tail twice, just as several puppies woke from their slumber, squeaked, and then started rooting for sustenance.

Heart sighed. "They truly are miracles, ain't so?"

"To be sure. You'll have to come back often to see how they grow. Before you know it, they'll be scampering everywhere and causing trouble!"

"*Jah*, but they'll be so cute, I doubt you'll mind. Are you going to keep any of them?"

"I'm afraid not. The puppies will bring me a good price. The money will be a nice addition to my savings account."

"I understand."

Heart stayed a few more minutes, but knew it was time to go home. She was getting hungry, plus there were treats to make before her father's mysterious guest arrived.

Just as she was about to leave, she caught sight of a cage in the corner. "What's that?"

"Hmm? Oh, that's Spike."

Heart walked closer and was startled to realize it was a pure white, rather stout rat. "Mary, why do you have a rat in your living room? And why does it have a name?"

"Well, the last woman I cared for passed away suddenly. She'd been a teacher or some such. This was her class's pet rat."

"I see." Of course, she didn't see at all.

Obviously reading her mind, Mary chuckled. "Spike isn't a sewer rat; he's a domesticated one."

"I didn't know there was such a thing."

"Oh, *jah*. Rats are popular pets. He's smart, cuddly, and a good companion. When I realized what her awful family planned to do to him—which was chop off his head—I couldn't let him stay."

Though Heart had never thought about keeping a rodent as a pet, she sure didn't like that idea, either. "That's horrible."

"What was sad was the inhumane way they were going to dispose of him." Her voice lowered. "He'd never done a thing to them, either. I was so upset, I took him home."

"Good for you." Unable to help herself, she shivered. "Poor thing."

"He's a *gut* pet, for sure and for certain. Spike knows his name, and when I let him out of the cage, he never goes far. Most of the time he simply crawls onto my lap while I read. He really is a sweetheart." Mary sighed. "The only problem is that I don't know what I'm going to do with him now."

"You don't want a pet rat?"

"I'm going to watch another patient starting on Monday. When I broached the subject of maybe bringing Spike and keeping him in his cage in my room, everyone in my patient's family had a fit. Why, one of the man's daughters said that he likely carried rabies."

Heart knew next to nothing about pet rats, but the daughter's words did seem rather harsh. "What are you going to do?"

"I don't know. That conversation just happened this morning. My neighbor has offered to watch Virginia and the pups for a few days, but he won't have the rat."

Heart took a longer look at Spike. He stared back. A lump formed in her throat. The little rat was studying her, almost with a look of longing. He needed a home.

She certainly had that.

"I'll take him," she blurted.

Mary turned away from the rodent and gaped at her. "What?"

"I'll give Spike a home. I mean, if you don't mind."

"Are you sure you want him?"

"Absolutely."

"But what about your father? I mean, won't Levi be upset?"

Heart was surprised that Mary knew her father's first name. But that was silly. Of course, she did. Apple Creek was a small community, and both of their families had lived there for some time.

Hoping she sounded more confident than she actually was, she said, "*Mei* father won't be upset at all. I'll keep Spike in my room. Plus, Daed is usually out in his workshop. He'll probably forget that there's even a rat living in our house." At least she hoped that was the case. Leaning down a bit, she carefully stuck a finger through the cage and gave Spike a tiny pet.

Mary clasped her hands together. "Heart, if you could give this rat a good home, I'd be so grateful."

"Consider it done. Ah, what does Spike eat?"

Hurrying over to a cabinet in her kitchen, Mary pulled out a plastic container. "Here's all of Spike's things. He loves his chew toys, and the roll of paper towels is so he can make a cozy nest." As she put all the items into a canvas bag, she added, "Rats are mighty clean, so be sure to change the shredded paper every week. Make sure his water bottle has fresh water, too. Now, to eat, he likes rat pellets and fresh fruit and vegetables." Smiling at the little creature, Mary softened her voice. "He especially loves strawberries."

"Spike loves strawberries?" She never would've guessed that.

"He enjoys being held and cuddling on your lap, too. But it might take a while for him to warm up to you enough to do that."

Spike was beginning to sound far more personable—and harder to keep hidden—than she'd realized. "Okay."

Mary chuckled. "If you have questions, you know where to come. I'll help you as much as I can."

"I'll keep that in mind." Thinking of her chores and that Spike was going to need to be cared for a bit, she stood up. "I think I should probably get on my way now."

It could've been her imagination, but Mary looked rather eager for Heart to be on her way. "There's a handle at the top of his cage. It's not heavy."

Next thing Heart knew, she was headed back home with a canvas bag on her shoulder and a rat cage in her arms. She was already regretting her decision, but consoled herself that a future pet-sitter needed to have at least one pet at home.

"I hope we'll become fast friends, Spike," she muttered. "I also hope and pray that you'll be easy to take care of."

Unfortunately, the rat didn't squeak in reassurance. Instead, she reckoned the little guy looked rather tense and worried.

And that was all she needed to know. Spike had lost his owner and now Mary. No doubt he was afraid she was going to be of the same mind as the terrible relatives and murder him.

"You and I are going to get along just fine," she said. "All you have to remember is that if my *daed* ever does realize you're in the house, he probably isn't going to be too happy about it. Don't worry, though. He can sound gruff, but his bark is worse than his bite."

As she walked up her driveway, her heart sank. Her father was standing in front of the house talking to a young man with brown hair. Both turned to her as she approached.

Inwardly she sighed. It seemed her father's surprise

guest had arrived. And, of course, he was as handsome as could be.

He and her father were both staring at Spike's cage as if it was about to combust.

It seemed her secret pet rat wasn't much of a secret anymore.

Chapter 3

All things considered, Clayton's first thirty minutes in the company of the famous Levi Beachy were nothing like he'd expected. Levi was known far and wide in the blacksmithing and ironworks world. Not only could he easily shoe a horse in record time, he excelled at producing true works of art. Some of the pieces he'd created had sold for thousands of dollars. People as far away as San Francisco commissioned pieces from him. Moreover, much to everyone's amazement, each client went to Levi's workshop to pick up the piece of art themselves.

Clayton's mentor, Garrett, had given him a great deal of advice while they were waiting for an *English* driver to pick him up and take him to Levi's workshop. Garrett had even cautioned Clayton to be respectful and do his best to listen well. And not to get discouraged too fast.

That advice had only made Clayton feel more uneasy. In addition to being a master craftsman, Levi was also known to be impatient and have quite a caustic tongue.

Even though Clayton hadn't been there long, he believed that the formidable man's reputation seemed to be right on the money. He was gruff, looked at his new apprentice as if he was an idiot, and acted as if simply being in the same room as Clayton was an inconvenience.

So that had been nerve-wracking.

However, on a positive note, Levi wasn't mean. And the projects he was working on fairly took Clayton's breath away.

But then things had gotten strange real fast. After muttering something about cereal treats, Levi took him into the house.

Curious about what the man could possibly be talking about, Clayton had followed him out of the barn and across the driveway to the house.

After telling Clayton that there was no need to remove his boots, they walked inside. The first stop was the kitchen, of course.

It looked the way he always had imagined his mother's kitchen would be—dishes in the sink, towels on the counter, and the makings of the midday meal next to the stove.

Looking perplexed, Levi drew to a stop and frowned. Then he stared at Clayton.

As seconds passed and it was obvious that Levi was waiting for something, Clayton blurted the only thing he could think of. "It's, ah, a right nice kitchen."

"*Nee*, it ain't. It's a mess."

The man looked so confused, Clayton kept talking. For some reason he had decided to stick up for the kitchen, even though he had very little experience with either kitchens or cleaning them. "It looks fine to me. Nothing out of the ordinary."

Levi's irritated look swung back to him. "It's out of the ordinary for this house," he barked. "And where's Heart?"

Clayton had no idea what he was talking about, so he just shrugged.

"Heart?" Levi yelled. "Heart! Where are ya?"

When several seconds passed, Clayton began to wonder if a comment was expected. "Heart doesn't seem to be here," he said at last.

Levi turned to face him. And blinked. "Let's go back outside. Maybe she's working in the henhouse."

As they walked back outside, Clayton thought he was finally putting two and two together. "Your wife's name is Heart?"

"No. My wife isn't here."

"I see." Of course, he didn't.

When the door closed behind them and they were standing on the gravel drive, Levi spoke again. "My daughter's name is Heart."

"Ah. Well, that is unusual."

"We didn't name her that. Her real name is Hazel."

Clayton was beginning to feel as if he'd stepped into

the middle of a very strange game—one where Levi
Beachy spoke in spurts and incomprehensible phrases
and he was supposed to discern their meanings. "Hazel."
When Levi raised his eyebrows, obviously looking for
more of a response, Clayton shoved his hands in his
pockets. "Ah."

That seemed to be all Levi needed.

"Hazel is a *gut* name. It's solid and normal." He
frowned. "The girl didn't care for it much, though.
Named herself Heart and there was no going back."

Given the man's forceful personality, Clayton was
stunned that the girl had gotten her way. "I see."

"*Ach*, it is what it is, you know?" Putting both hands
on his hips, he looked around the lawn. "I have to tell
ya that I'm not sure what is going on. I really wanted
those monster cookies. Heart said she'd have them.
What time is it?"

"Ah, about two, I think."

"Oh. That's the reason."

Clayton wasn't sure whether Levi was worried
about the girl or just annoyed that she wasn't working
in the kitchen. Though she sounded like such a young,
needy thing, he reckoned that her father's worry was
probably justified.

He was just about to offer to help Levi search the
grounds when a woman appeared at the end of the driveway. As she came closer, he was aware of two things:
Heart Beachy was no wayward child, not even close.
Secondly, Heart was the prettiest thing he'd ever seen
in his life. She had light blond hair, a slim figure, a

lovely face, and bright blue eyes. It was everything he could do not to gape.

"Is, ah, that your daughter?" he asked. Just to be sure.

"*Jah*. That there is Heart." Levi frowned. "I don't know what she's carrying, though."

Realizing that the two of them were standing there staring at Heart when she could likely use a hand, Clayton started forward. "May I help ya carry that?" he called out.

Her eyes widened. "Are you my father's guest?"

"I am. Well, I'm here because I'm Levi's new apprentice." When she continued to stare at him, he smiled slightly. "My name is Clayton. Clayton Glick. And you're Heart."

"*Jah*."

"I'm sorry, I came out to help you, yet here I am, still watching you carry that cage." He held out his hands.

"It's all right. You don't have to carry it. I've gotten this far on my own."

"It's my pleasure." Gazing into the container, he was stunned to see a rather rotund white rat inside. It was staring at him intently, as if it was trying to measure Clayton's worth.

It was one of the strangest things he'd encountered that week. Well, that, the fact that Levi spoke in half sentences, and learning that Levi Beachy had a beautiful daughter who'd named herself Heart.

He gestured to the rodent. "So, what is this?"

"This is Spike."

"He looks like a rat."

"That's because he is." Her lips pressed together.

"Is he your pet?" Maybe she went for walks with the cage? It sounded unlikely, but he was beginning to think that anything was possible on this farm.

"He is now."

"Heart, I went inside, but you weren't there," her father called out.

Staring at her *daed*, Heart released a long, rather drawn-out sigh. "Take Spike for me, please?" She handed Clayton the cage and then squared her shoulders as if she was walking into battle. "I'd better go get this over with."

When she started forward, Clayton fell into step beside her. He felt a bit foolish, but what else could he do?

When they stopped in front of Levi, Heart said, "Daed, I understand that you're gonna be having an apprentice."

"I am. It was a shame that you weren't here to greet him, though."

"I told you I was going for a walk. Remember?"

"Hmm? Oh, *jah*." He cleared his throat. "You left the kitchen a mess."

"I'll clean it in a little while."

"And there are no cookies."

"I'll make those, too."

"If you have time, that is." There was a touch of sarcasm in his voice.

Heart crossed her arms. "You asked me to provide a

snack but I haven't had time to make it yet. It's barely two o'clock."

Clayton hid a smile. The girl obviously had a lot of practice sparring with Levi. She didn't look cowed in the slightest.

Only then did Levi seem to notice that Clayton was standing beside them holding a big cage in his arms. "What is that?"

"This is Spike. I now have a pet rat."

Levi's eyebrows snapped together. "You canna have a rat. They carry diseases."

"Not Spike. He's a fancy rat."

Levi folded his arms over his chest. "Given the fact that he has a big cage, toys, and my new apprentice is carrying him around, I'd say that he is a mite too fancy."

Heart giggled. "Fancy rats are a type of rat. Like Clydesdales are a type of horse."

"Whatever Spike is, he canna stay." Levi huffed. "I don't want to live with a rat."

"I'm sorry, but he needs a home. He's so small, I don't think he'll be much trouble at all. You'll hardly notice he's here."

"I'll notice."

"Mary Miller asked us to take him, Daed."

And just like that, everything about the formidable blacksmith changed. His expression softened and his voice did, too. "This rat is from Mary?"

She smiled. "It is. She told me about Spike, and I offered to take him. You know I don't want to go back on my word."

"I reckon not. But . . . why?"

"I'll tell you the whole story at supper." Turning to Clayton, she asked, "Will you be joining us?"

After glancing at Levi, who shrugged, Clayton nodded. "I would love to join you. *Danke.*" Besides, his apprenticeship was supposed to include room and board.

Her soft smile changed into a bright grin. "You're welcome. It's the least I can do, given that you're carrying around my pet rat and all. Will you bring him inside for me?"

"*Jah*, sure." After he took two steps, he looked back at Levi. The man hadn't moved from where he was standing. His arms were still folded across his chest, and he looked mighty perplexed.

Feeling the need to say something—the man truly did look as if he'd just had the rug pulled out from under his feet—Clayton called out, "I'll be right back, Levi."

"Hmm? Oh, *jah.* Take your time," Levi said. After studying Clayton a moment longer, he turned toward the barn. "I have something I need to take care of, anyway."

Uh-oh. Was Levi irritated with him? So far, he wasn't making much of a good first impression.

"I don't think your father is pleased with me."

When the man was out of sight, Heart chuckled. "Don't fret, Clayton. He's not mad. My father wanders off all the time."

"You sure about that?"

"Very sure. You canna take it personally. My father is gruff and a bit surly, but not mean. You'll get used to it in time." Her expression softened. "Especially if you decide to work for him, yes?"

"Right." He returned her smile, but he couldn't help but think it was a shame that she had become used to it. A girl like her should be doted on. Or, at the very least, not be ignored.

Looking at the cage, she brightened again. "Let's go inside and see what Spike thinks of his new home."

Clayton followed her to the house. He was no rat, but if he had to guess, he'd reckon that the animal was going to like his new home just fine.

He certainly did.

Chapter 4

Glad for the privacy of his barn workshop, Levi closed the heavy oak door behind him. Out of habit, he leaned against the wood and breathed deep. The old wood creaked in protest at his weight, but held firm. Just as it always did.

Giving in, he closed his eyes.

The workshop was his safe place. He'd hidden in there when he doubted himself and his artistic abilities and didn't want Katie to worry. He'd found comfort against the old door when his dear wife got weaker, and he wasn't sure if he had enough strength to care for either himself or Heart. Now, even when he wasn't worried or upset, Levi often found himself taking a few moments simply to let his guard down. Though he reckoned that might not be the healthiest course of action, it had become a habit.

As the faint scent of acrid smoke and horse surrounded him, the familiar aromas relaxed his muscles. Within a few seconds he felt centered again.

He was thankful, since he was surely in need of support. It had been a relief when Heart had seemed just fine with Clayton lending her a hand. He needed a few moments to pull himself together.

His darling, hardworking, very earnest daughter had brought home a rat. It was named Spike and it was going to be Heart's new pet. And his as well, because although his lovely, hardworking daughter always assumed he didn't pay attention to anything beyond metal, fire, and the work in this room . . . he was still very aware of other things. He made sure that Heart had everything she needed, even when he couldn't provide it.

Pleased that no one was around to witness it, he chuckled. The sound, altogether unfamiliar in this space, reverberated around the walls and seemed to echo. That was a fanciful thought, to be sure, but he didn't mind.

Instead of embarrassing Levi, his chuckle lightened his spirits and reminded him that he was still alive. Not just in body, but in his soul as well. For a while there—after Katie met Jesus in Heaven—he hadn't been sure that was the case. For weeks he'd been barely a shell of a man and had relied on his daughter to take care of his every need.

Katie would've chided him for that.

He would've deserved the lecture, too.

But now, here he was, laughing because of a certain white rat with a small weight problem.

No. While that rat was rather cute—in a strange sort of rodent way—it was where the rat had come from that had his insides tied up in knots and his mood swinging to and fro. Spike had belonged to Mary.

Mary Miller, who'd once cared for Katie so generously.

Mary Miller, whom he'd begun to notice more and more in spite of his best intentions not to.

He sat down. The woman was constantly amusing him with her generous spirit and willingness to help everyone around her. She had become a bright light in his world. He liked everything about her. Her rather bold habit of sharing unasked-for opinions, her tentativeness when she received a compliment, the way she cared for both animals and her charges. In spite of their best intentions, they'd become friends.

It hadn't started out that way. He'd only gotten to know her when Katie became ill and she'd come over to help him tend to his wife. Thinking back to how he'd treated Mary, Levi winced. He'd been so torn up with grief and despair, he'd barely been civil. As the days and weeks passed, he'd eventually become far more polite and then almost kind. However, his mind hadn't been on anything to do with friendship. His dear wife had been dying and he'd felt as if he'd been losing a piece of himself with each dying breath she took.

That had been four years ago.

As the years passed, Levi had only spoken to Mary

Miller in passing. Sometimes he'd nod in her direction when their eyes met in church. Every once in a while he'd even unbend enough to ask her how she was.

It had been enough. He'd been busy attempting to put his life together and look out for Heart. Mary was helping other men and women either recover from surgery or spend their last weeks on earth with a measure of dignity. And then they'd ended up both eating at the diner one night and started talking. He'd gone so far as to join her at her table when a couple came in and there was nowhere for him to sit by himself.

Mary had been surprised by his company, but hadn't seemed upset to have it. He had felt awkward, but had eventually relaxed. They'd sat together for over an hour. He, who barely even took fifteen minutes to consume a Thanksgiving dinner!

Ever since then, he'd been smitten with the widow Mary Miller. He just didn't know what to do about it.

Heart's claiming of her rat seemed like the perfect reason to go pay Mary a call. He could hardly wait to give her grief about handing off the rodent—and hear her response.

"Hello?"

Realizing his assistant had returned, Levi picked up a broom and started sweeping the floor. "Come in, Clayton."

"I'm sorry that I disappeared like that. It looked like Heart had her hands full."

"Ack. You were right, she did. Don't ever be sorry for giving my daughter a hand. She's a *gut* girl and deserves your kindness." Glancing at the man, who was still standing near the door, he asked, "So, in what room did Heart decide to house the rat?"

"She put Spike in her bedroom."

"In her bedroom? Ah." That was a disappointment. He had kind of been looking forward to getting to know the critter.

He had no idea why.

Clayton gave him a sideways look, letting Levi know that his disappointment had been noted. "I believe Heart thought you'd prefer him in there with her."

He continued to sweep. "I reckon I would, though it don't really make a lot of difference to me one way or the other. I'm not inside all that much. Why, I bet I'll even forget it's in the *haus*."

"If so, you're a better man than me. Even though Heart tried to tell me all about the rodent's fine qualities, I would still be afraid that it would get out and start nesting in a slipper or some such."

Levi turned to him. "I hope you didn't tell Heart that. She might start to worry."

"No, sir. I did not." Looking embarrassed for speaking his mind, Clayton added, "Please forgive me for being so bold."

"There isn't anything to forgive." Levi chuckled. "You're entitled to speak your mind. I respect that. It's just that, ah, Heart has a soft soul. I try not to hurt her feelings if I can help it."

Reminding himself that they were talking about rat ownership and not courtship, Levi cleared his throat. "For the record, though, the girl does seem to be quite taken with . . . What was the critter's name again?" Of course, he knew it, but there was no way he would let Clayton realize just how much he was actually aware of what went on with his daughter.

"Spike. Its name is Spike."

"Ah, yes. Well, she already seems fond of it." And now . . . he should probably speak about something besides rats and his daughter's tender heart. "I want to welcome ya here again. How about I give you a tour of my shop and then you can get settled in your room?"

"*Jah.* That sounds good."

"Also, before I forget to say it, don't be shy about asking me questions. I, uh, may not always act very open to talk, but I am. Working with fire can be dangerous, ain't so?"

"*Jah.*" Clayton's expression was serious.

"I'm glad you are aware of how dangerous blacksmithing can be. It's better to work careful and slow instead of too fast and careless. If you get hurt, it will cost me time and money."

"I understand." Clayton looked down at the ground, where he'd deposited both a large duffel and a heavy-looking backpack. "Would you like me to take notes?"

"You can if you'd like, but I don't think you're gonna need to study what I tell ya all that much."

Clayton swallowed. "I understand."

The boy was nervous. Deciding to conduct only a cursory tour, then give him time to get settled and gain his bearings, Levi stepped in front of the forge. "This here is the forge, of course. And these are my many tools. I have them divided into two groups. Everything for shoeing horses is on the left and for *mei* art is on the right."

"You never use the same tool for both?"

"Not really."

"Why?"

"Well, now, I guess I never really asked myself that question. I suppose the main reason is that in my mind the two jobs are two separate things. It never seemed right to me to make a thing of beauty out of something that's been used on the bottom end of a horse."

"I see."

Levi wasn't sure if there was something to "see" or not, but he supposed it didn't matter. Walking over to the back of the area, he opened the farthest door. It was a large space, easily double the size of his workshop. It was clean as a whistle and had six roomy stalls and several additional posts to tie up horses. A couple of wooden stools were stacked in a corner so anyone who brought a horse in could sit down while they waited.

Glancing at Clayton, he noticed that the young man looked impressed. It was prideful, but Levi was pleased about that. It had taken him years to arrange this space to his liking—almost as long as it had taken him to develop his reputation.

Pushing away those thoughts, he headed into the main part of the barn. Becket, his Tennessee Walker, poked his head out to say hello.

After greeting the horse and taking a moment to rub the animal's velvet nose, he spoke to Clayton. "This here is Becket, my buggy horse. He's friendly, but an independent sort. Becket, this man is Clayton. He's all right."

Becket allowed Clayton to pet his mane, but only for a moment. Then he turned back to the confines of his roomy stall. Passing a few empty stalls, Levi continued the tour. "Obviously, this here is where men bring in their horses." He pointed to a pair of doors that opened wide to a side drive. "Customers can come in this way without having to worry about scaring their horses. Don't forget to leave at least one stall in between Becket and the customers' horses. Becket ain't a big fan of company."

"*Jah*, I'm getting that impression."

Opening another door, Levi pointed to a small, rather jumbled workbench and pegboard. "This is where I keep the tack."

"I see."

Seeing it from a visitor's eyes, Levi realized that it looked exactly like what it was: a forgotten room in a busy life. "It looks a bit rough, don't it? Maybe you could clean it sometime soon."

"Yes, sir."

After closing the door, Levi showed Clayton a utility sink and the hose for the horses' water.

Clayton seemed to be cataloging everything in his head. "About how many horses do you shoe a week?" he asked.

"A week?" He ran a hand along the beard that he kept shorn. "It varies. Sometimes three or four, sometimes a dozen or so."

"How do you plan for it?"

"You can't plan for a horse needing a new shoe. If they need one, their owner brings them in.

"Come on back." He led the way into the main workshop, then opened up the second door. "Here's the other part of my work."

The setup here was a bit different. There was a small hallway that led to a sitting area, complete with a restroom and leather chairs and couches.

Clayton whistled low. "This is fancy."

"I come to understand that some of my customers travel a long way to see everything in person. They need a little bit more than I had available." He walked into the last room. "And here's the gallery."

All the walls were pale gray. The floor was cement. One could see the rafters on the ceiling. Bars of spotlights were attached to some of them.

Below were cream-colored stone pedestals of various heights. And on top of about seven of them were iron pieces of art that he'd designed, forged, polished, and eventually decided to part with.

Clayton's expression was filled with awe. "May I walk around?"

"Of course, man. Nothing is made to stare at from a distance." He motioned with his hands. "Take your time."

He remained where he was as he watched Clayton walk a full circle around each piece.

"These are incredible," he murmured. "I had no idea that some of the pieces were so big. Some of them are so intricately designed and detailed, it's hard to believe they're made of metal."

"Jah?"

"Pictures in a book or on the Internet don't do your work justice. It's all beautiful. Awe-inspiring, really."

"I appreciate your words." He didn't believe in massaging his pride, but the boy's words did feel good.

"You're welcome." Walking to his side, Clayton said, "I'm looking forward to learning from you, Levi."

"I hope I can teach you the skills you are hoping to learn. Are you wanting to shoe horses or pursue art?"

"Art, one day. For now, I'll plan to do a good job with everything practical."

He nodded. "That is a good plan. It's always been my opinion that the two go hand in hand. One learns patience shoeing horses. That patience has come in handy when I'm working with some of my pieces. I reckon you might come to the same conclusion."

"Yes, sir."

Clayton was standing so still and stiff, Levi thought he could be taken for a piece of ironwork himself. He needed to relax, but Levi wasn't sure how to get him to do that. Inspiring warm and cozy conversation wasn't exactly something he'd ever done. "Let's go to your living space now."

Clayton grabbed his belongings and followed him.

Levi climbed the old ladder first. When Clayton moved to follow on his heels, he called down for him to wait. "This ladder's almost a hundred years old. I wouldn't trust it with our combined weight."

"All right."

After pulling himself up, Levi moved to the side, taking care to remain in a half crouch. "Come up now, but watch your head. The ceiling is lower than I remember." He actually couldn't recall the last time he'd been in the loft.

Clayton climbed up and deposited his duffel bag on the floor. A cloud of dust puffed up.

Hmm. The space was dirtier than he'd remembered as well.

Clayton didn't say anything, but Levi could practically feel the young man's obvious dismay.

"So this is the loft. It's not much. I know that."

Almost standing—the ceiling really was rather low—the two men surveyed the space. There was an old twin bed pushed against the wall. An old stool was nearby. That was it. The mattress was bare and the metal bedframe appeared rickety. There wasn't even a braided rug on the floor to warm things up. It was also dark. Glad he had a small flashlight in his pocket, Levi pulled it out. Clicking the button, he shined the light around the area.

There were a whole lot more spiderwebs than he remembered. Two beetles scurried out of the way. And . . . dare he admit it? There was the annoyed squeak of a mouse.

It was truly an awful place to house a new apprentice. So awful, Levi realized he was embarrassed about it. Though he could practically feel Katie's gentle hand on his shoulder, chiding him for being thoughtless, he attempted to salvage his pride.

"Hmm. It seems I forgot to prepare this room for you."

One second passed. Clayton cleared his throat. "It's fine. I can clean it up."

"Yes." Turning to face the boy, Levi nodded. "You can take the broom up here."

A flash of skepticism flashed in Clayton's eyes before he blinked. "*Danke*. Do you have sheets for the bed? And, uh, maybe a towel?"

"A towel?"

"Yes. You know, so I could shower." When Levi simply stared at him, Clayton added, "I'd like to be able to take a shower every day."

The young man's voice now had an edge to it. And, perhaps, a bit of sarcasm. And who could blame him? Pushing back his embarrassment again, he stuffed his hands in his pockets. "Of course, you'll be needing to shower. Since there's no bathroom here, you may use one of the bathrooms in the house. We have three." Once again, he could feel Katie's disapproval.

"Danke."

"And as far as towels and sheets and stuff . . . I believe everything you need is in the *haus*. Heart knows where it all is. Ask her and she'll show ya."

"Okay."

Hating how uncomfortable he felt, Levi turned off the flashlight and crawled to the ladder. "Right. I'll let you get to it, then. You have the rest of the day to settle in. Maybe go into town and explore if you'd like. It ain't too far. Barely a mile. Now, um, unless you need something else, I've got an errand to run. Do you need something?"

"*Nee*, Levi."

"*Gut.* We'll get started in the morning. Come inside the kitchen at six for breakfast," he said, making no mention of dinner. Just as he stepped down on the ladder, he paused. "All right?"

"I'll be in your kitchen at six."

"*Gut.* Oh, and here," he said, setting the flashlight on the floor. "You'll be needing this."

Glad that Clayton remained silent, Levi climbed down the ladder, checked that the fire in the forge was almost out, and exited the barn. At last.

The cool, crisp air was a welcome change. It felt refreshing. Cleansing. He breathed deep, enjoying the way the cold air felt as it entered his lungs.

Only when chill bumps formed on his arms did he turn toward the house. Inside, he turned on the kitchen sink, found a scrub brush, and worked on his hands. It was almost impossible to remove the stains from his nail beds, but he did the best he could.

Then, before he could talk himself out of it, he put on a clean shirt, grabbed a pair of gloves, and then walked back outside. The brisk temperature greeted him again. After securing a few buttons on his coat, he pulled on his gloves and then slipped on a pair of sunglasses.

For some reason everything seemed brighter.

Chapter 5

After Heart left, Mary let Virginia outside to do her business and stretch her legs. Then, while Virginia ate some food and took a rest on the rug in front of the fire, she took care of the puppies' basket. Soiled and shredded newspaper was thrown out and new was put in. The worn, stained blanket was exchanged for a new one, and each tiny pup was carefully inspected and gently rubbed. One by one, she placed them on the clean blanket. When the last was situated, Virginia returned.

"Your puppies are doing well, girl," Mary said as she rubbed the retriever's favorite spot behind her ears. "You should be proud."

Virginia's soft eyes looked at her adoringly before inspecting each pup.

Mary chuckled at the way Virginia made sure to check all five. "Always a mother, hmm? Can't trust anyone's word with your children, can ya?"

When a knock sounded on the door, Mary was surprised. She hadn't expected anyone today. Of course, she hadn't known young Heart Beachy was going to visit, either. The girl's visit—and her willingness to take Spike home with her—had been a lovely and welcome surprise.

When Mary opened the door to greet the new visitor, her stomach sank. Levi, clad in a thick wool coat, black felt hat, and heavy-looking boots, was standing on her welcome mat. As usual, he wasn't smiling.

Actually, he looked irritated.

That could only mean one thing: Spike's appearance in his home had not gone over well.

Since there was nothing to do but figuratively grasp the bull by the horns, she straightened her spine a little bit and lifted her chin. Levi might be huge and scary, but she had a rat to look after. "Where is he?"

Slowly Levi blinked. "Who are you talking about?"

"Spike, of course."

"The rat?"

"Of course. Where is his cage?"

A line formed in between his dark blond brows. "Why would I have brought Spike back here? I thought you gave him to Heart."

All her worst fears came to life. "Oh, my word. Levi, did you kill him?"

His eyes widened in shock before a look of pure irritation appeared. "Step aside, Mary Miller. I believe we need to talk."

"No, we do not. There isn't a thing—"

"That's where you are wrong." Obviously deciding he'd had enough of waiting, Levi reached out, grasped her shoulders, and moved her to the side.

He wasn't rough, and his grip on her shoulders hadn't been tight. Since that was the case, why was she feeling a little off-kilter? Was it because of the burst of winter air he'd brought inside with him? Or the slight scent of fire and leather that seemed to permeate his very being?

"Please remove your hands."

Levi immediately complied. With a frown he glanced down at his hands. "I didn't hurt ya, did I?" Looking even more worried, he said, "I know my hands are rough. Sometimes I don't realize my strength. You know the last thing I would ever want—"

He really was afraid he'd bruised her. "Levi, stop. It's okay. Really. You didn't hurt me." She might hate that he'd murdered Spike, but she wasn't going to accuse him of something he didn't do.

"You could have simply asked me to move out of the doorway, however. I follow directions fairly well."

Not looking cowed—not even a little bit—Levi closed the door behind him. "I could've asked ya, but I was afraid you would refuse my request. Then what would I have done?"

Even though his words almost made sense, she paid them no mind. She was too upset about the rat. "I don't

know why I would listen to you when you thought
nothing about hurting Spike. And how could you do
that to Heart? She has a tender soul."

"I know she does." He rolled his eyes. "Mary, you
are a piece of work. I might be gruff and work with
metal and fire, but I haven't started killing pets yet."
His blue eyes—such a surprise to find in his hard, very
masculine features—flashed with something that
looked like a mixture of both amusement and exasperation. "Why have you decided I'm a rat killer?"

She was starting to think that she'd gotten this all
wrong. It was mortifying. "Um . . ."

He unbuttoned his coat and shrugged it off. "Worse,
do ya really think I would kill your pet rat, then walk
over here to tell you about it?"

She did not want to notice how broad his chest was
or how his biceps filled out the sleeves of his blue
shirt.

Which matched his eyes so perfectly.

She took a deep breath. "Well . . ."

"What kind of monster do you think I am?"

"Spike is all right?" Her voice was strained and
breathless, whether because she was getting treated to
a very up close and personal view of Levi or because
she was completely embarrassed, she didn't know.

"Of course, he is. Last I heard, Heart had him situated in her room. By now, he's eating rat food or whatever you told Heart to feed him. The creature is no
doubt counting his blessings that he's now a part of my
daughter's world."

His eyes were filled with hurt. She'd hurt his feelings.

What to say? "I don't think you're too rough. I certainly don't think you're a monster. I never have."

"Then why did you jump to such a conclusion?"

She wasn't sure. She needed to make amends, and fast. Without asking she pulled his coat out of Levi's hands and hung it on the hook next to the door. "Come sit down, Levi." She gestured to the sitting area. "I'm getting tired of looking up at you."

"What about my boots?"

"What about them?"

"Heart always complains about me tracking in dirt."

Looking at his boots, which were somewhere between dirty and filthy, Mary inwardly flinched. However, as much as she might enjoy a clean floor, she was not going to sit with a man who wore no boots. That felt too personal. "You are fine."

He sat down, leaving a telltale trail behind him. When he frowned at the mess, it was almost amusing.

"May I get you something to drink? I have some fresh cider."

"That sounds real nice. *Danke*."

Glad to have a moment to regain her composure, she poured two glasses of cider, then added five gingersnap cookies to a plate. When she returned, he was craning his neck to watch Virginia and the puppies.

"Would you like to see them?"

"I would. That is, if you don't think she'll mind?"

"She won't mind."

He was crossing the room to the whelping bed before she could complete her whole sentence.

"Ah, look at them." His voice was gentle and reverent.

Her heart skipped a little beat. Turning to the refrigerator, she replaced the bottle of cider. "They're adorable."

"Perfect." When Virginia looked up at him, he knelt down on one knee and held out a hand. "You should be proud, Virginia. They are very handsome."

As if on cue, one of them squeaked and then squirmed, obviously trying to get out from the puppy pile. Levi leaned forward, obviously anxious to help, but afraid to upset Virginia.

"You might ought to give that one a hand," she said.

Levi stilled. "You don't think Virginia will mind?"

"I think she'll be real pleased not to have to move them herself. Motherhood can be exhausting, you know."

"I'd forgotten you have a child. A son, yes?"

"Yes. But he's a man." He was also *English*, married, and long gone.

With gentle hands Levi carefully moved the pups, chuckling as the one who was fussing froze, then relaxed in his palm. After he set it back down, he stood up and returned to the couch. "I always forget how small they are."

"I didn't know you had dogs."

"I haven't. Not for a long while. I was always too busy with work. Plus, Katie wasn't one for animals."

"What about you?" she asked as she set their glasses on the table.

"Me? I've always been fond of them. Heart gets her love of animals naturally."

After bringing over a plate of cookies, Mary sat down. Levi lingered for a moment, then joined her.

When their eyes met, she knew she owed him an apology. "Uh, Levi, about earlier. I'm very sorry."

He stared at her a moment longer.

Ah, those blue eyes of his were going to be the death of her! It felt like he could see too much. Which seemed to make her talk too much.

"You see, I . . . Well, I couldn't imagine a reason for you to stop by unless it was to complain about the rat and give him back. When I didn't see the cage, I jumped to the wrong conclusion. I am sorry. I didn't mean to offend."

His whole expression shuttered. "Okay." He swallowed. "I didn't come over to complain about your fancy rat. Heart is already smitten with the creature, and I dare say it will soon be mutual if Spike ain't already feeling fond of her, too."

"I'm glad you told me that." She leaned forward. "Is that why you came over, Levi?"

"Yes, I suppose it is."

"I'm glad you did."

He got to his feet. "I should probably get going."

She sure wished he wouldn't. "Don't you want to drink your cider and eat a cookie? They're gingersnaps."

To her surprise, he sat down again. After she joined him, Levi closed his eyes, said a quick prayer, and then picked up his glass and sipped.

"The cider is delicious, Mary."

That was the thing about Levi Beachy. He was a mess of contradictions. He was the biggest man she knew and twice as gruff, but never harsh. Actually, she'd never heard him raise his voice to anyone. Likely, it was because he had no need to. Between his size and his continual scowl, most people in the area were anxious to do what he wanted and get out of his way.

But there was also something about him. An aura or an attitude or . . . something special. Whatever it was, it had always drawn her to him like a moth to a flame.

"You know I didn't press the apples, Levi. I bought it at the market."

"You are serving it. That is enough."

Unable to argue with his logic, she inclined her head. "Perhaps."

Levi studied her for a long moment.

Feeling bold, Mary stared right back. And just like that, she was pulled into his gaze. Next thing she knew, she was admiring his eyes, noticing the faint specks of gold close to the pupils. They were beautiful. Mary would have believed they were wasted on such a masculine man except that they added a note of beauty to an otherwise taciturn and rough demeanor.

They made him approachable.

After too short a time, Levi turned his head. A second later, he picked up the glass in a meaty paw and drank the rest of its contents in one gulp.

"Levi?" She didn't know what to say, but Mary felt she should say something. The tension flowing between them was tangible.

"I need to leave," he blurted. He stood up. Then reached out and grabbed two cookies. "My new assistant just arrived this afternoon. He's probably wondering what to do now. Or . . . Heart is wondering what to do with him."

That made her smile. Mary knew enough about Heart to be aware that she might have inherited her mother's beauty, but she had gleaned more than just a pair of blue eyes from her father. "Your daughter is nothing if not competent."

He smiled. "She is that." Reaching for his coat, he pulled it back on, taking care not to crumble the cookies as he did. Just as he reached the door, he looked back at her. "Are you all right, Mary? Do you need anything?"

Her insides twinged before she firmly tamped down her feelings. "What would I need?"

"It's December. The weather ain't bad right now, but it will be. Do you have wood? I'd hate for you to be cold."

"I do have wood. But thank you."

"I'll stop by in a day or two and chop some more for ya."

"If you stop by, I'll make sure I have some cider for you."

The corners of his lips almost curved up before he turned and walked out the door.

The moment it closed, she felt as if half the oxygen in the room had wandered out as well.

From her box in the corner Virginia groaned as she stretched.

"I feel the same way, Virginia. It's feeling rather empty and cold in here all of a sudden, isn't it?" She had a feeling not even a roaring fire in the fireplace was going to warm it up, either.

Chapter 6

Heart wasn't sure where her father had run off to, but she supposed it didn't matter. She had a dozen things to do around the house. If he was nearby, he'd only get in the way.

Glancing at the kitchen clock, she winced. The day was passing like lightning. She needed to finish preparing the evening meal or it wouldn't be on the table at five o'clock, the way her father liked it to be.

Glad to remember that she'd transferred some chicken from the freezer to the refrigerator the day before, she was pleased that she'd decided to make chicken stew with fresh biscuits. The meal would be warm and filling—the perfect antidote for such a chilly and gray day.

She'd already chopped up the carrots, onions, and potatoes. Soon she'd braise the chicken, and then set it on the stove to cook. Served with biscuits, it would be a warm and filling meal. There would be a lot of it, too. Especially if, say, Clayton was in need of something to eat.

She stilled, thinking about it. Where was Clayton planning to eat this evening? Of course, her father had left without letting her know. Likely, he hadn't even thought about his apprentice's stomach.

She groaned. But, truly, where else would their new addition eat? Unless someone was planning to pick him up, Clayton was stuck on the farm.

"Daed, you'd test the patience of a saint!" she told the empty room.

Deciding to start cooking the stew early, since she was mentally stewing about supper, anyway, Heart pulled out the pot and began putting in the vegetables with quick, precise movements.

Two sharp knocks at the back door brought her up short.

Guessing who it was, she hurried to open it. "Hiya, Clayton."

"Hiya, Heart. I'm sorry to bother you."

He looked unhappy and awkward. "You aren't a bother. Come in."

"Danke." He followed her into the kitchen. "Ah, it's warm in here."

"It is. Probably far warmer than in the barn."

"Oh, the barn's okay." Shrugging, he let his gaze stray to the pile of carrots and potatoes in the stew pot. "You were cooking."

"*Nee*. Just putting everything in the pot. How may I help you?"

"I, uh, came to ask if I might use the toilet."

"Excuse me?"

Obviously embarrassed, Clayton stared at a point across the room. "The barn has no bathroom. I guess I drank a lot of water earlier."

He was apologizing for being human. That father of hers! Would he ever stop to think of anything but horseshoes and artwork?

Mortified by how unwelcoming they must seem, she closed her eyes and said a quick prayer. She needed all the help she could get to make things better for Clayton. When she gazed at him again, she realized that his eyes were almost a caramel color. So striking.

Not that it mattered at the moment.

"Oh, my word. Of course. I'm so sorry. It's down the hall, to your right."

"*Danke*." He bent to remove his boots.

"You don't need to—"

"I do," he said as he toed them off. "I don't want to create more work than you already have."

After he disappeared down the hall, she washed her hands and thought about his living conditions. An awful, sick feeling started to nest in the bottom of her stomach. Her father had no doubt stuck his new apprentice in the loft.

That dirty, dark, bug-infested room in the loft. Where mice likely lived. And not fancy ones like Spike, either. Feral, sneaky mice who would be exploring his things while he was attempting to sleep.

It wasn't going to do.

What felt like thirty seconds later, Clayton appeared again. *"Danke,"* he said. "Sorry for the trouble."

"It wasn't any trouble. Also, you don't ever need to thank me for letting you use the restroom, Clayton."

Standing in front of her, he fidgeted again. "Since I've already interrupted ya, would you mind letting me know where the linens are? And maybe some cleaning supplies?"

This was getting worse and worse. "Because you need to clean your room."

"Well, yes."

Heart figured she could do two things: either continue this farce and give the poor man sheets and a dustcloth . . . or do the right thing.

"Clayton, we have an extra bedroom here in the *haus*. You may stay there."

"Nee."

"I insist." When he looked ready to argue again, she added, "That loft in the barn . . . Well, it ain't good up there."

White teeth flashed, but he shook his head again. "I'll be fine."

"No. No, you won't. Like I said, it's empty. You should sleep in the guest bedroom instead."

"Your father won't be pleased."

"I'll take care of him."

"You don't understand. I need this apprenticeship. Plus, it's December. If he throws me out, I won't have anywhere to go."

He would be homeless? Where was his family? Why was he all alone? Not liking the answer to those questions, she felt her resolve deepen.

"Clayton, I think it would be best if you understood something about my father. He's a good man. A gifted man. I love him."

He clasped his hands behind his back. "Of course, you do."

"However, even though I love him very much, Levi Beachy doesn't always live in the real world. When my mother was alive, she helped with that. He listened to her, no matter what. But ever since she went to Heaven, he's preferred to live in his own world of horses and iron and fire and art. He didn't think about your room because he doesn't notice that I clean his room and make sure he always has clean sheets and blankets."

She stepped closer. "That is why I know that you need to stay in the house. If my father was the type of man to think about something as mundane as a bedroom, he would know, without any doubt, that you should not be staying in the barn."

"That is kind of you."

"Then it's settled, yes?" She smiled.

"Not quite. Your father left. I'll talk to him about it when he returns."

"Trust me, he's not going to want to talk about your sleeping arrangements. He's going to be wanting supper."

"But—"

"Clayton, I know I'm right. Now let's stop arguing. Let me show you your room in here, and then you can move your things." She headed down the hall before he could take the opportunity to argue again.

When she opened the guest bedroom door, she heard his footsteps behind her. "Here we are," she said. "I think you'll be much more comfortable here."

He stood in the doorway. "It's mighty fine."

She had to agree. It was a lovely room indeed. Her mother had picked out a bedroom set in pine. It was stained a deep brown and the grain of the wood felt like butter. The bed was queen-sized, had flannel sheets and a down comforter under an intricately pieced quilt in a wedding ring pattern in shades of gray. On the floor was Heart's favorite item in the room, a warm, soft sheepskin rug. Its color had always reminded her of melted vanilla ice cream. It was pristine, beautiful, and totally unsuitable for a blacksmith's life. Mamm had forbidden her father to go near it.

Stepping inside, Heart beckoned Clayton to follow. "The fireplace in here works and the door leads to the bathroom you just used. I think you'll find it to be far more comfortable than the barn."

Clayton was staring at the rug as if it was a living thing. "Heart, this is far too nice. I could get something dirty."

"If you do, you may help clean it. Ain't so?"

"I suppose."

"Go get your things, Clayton. I don't have more time to argue. My father likes to eat his meals on time."

He stepped toward the door, then stopped to look back at her. "Heart?"

"Jah?"

"I . . . I just wanted to thank you for this. And, um, even though I'm a stranger to you, I want to reassure you that I would never take advantage of either you or your father."

He looked so earnest.

"That never crossed my mind," she said softly. "Please stop worrying about this room. Everything will be fine."

"I'll return soon with my things."

"Good. And when you do, don't bother to knock. You're no longer a guest. Why, you're practically part of the family." She waved a hand.

"I'm a long way from that, Heart."

"Not to me. Why, you're almost like a brother, or an uncle, or something. Right?"

"Jah." Something flickered in his eyes. If she had to guess, she'd say that he didn't completely agree with her statement.

She could understand that.

After all, there was something about him that made her think of far different things from brothers and uncles.

No, she didn't think about him that way at all.

Chapter 7

He was going to be released from his apprenticeship before it even had a chance to begin. Clayton was as certain of that as he was that steel had to be heated to over a thousand degrees before it could bend.

And who could blame Levi, anyway? He'd brought on an apprentice to help his horseshoeing business. Business that he likely didn't even need.

At the children's home Garrett had made no bones about that.

It seemed the hard-as-iron man had a soft spot hidden carefully inside him and had taken in Clayton out of the goodness of his heart. It hadn't taken Clayton longer than two seconds to realize that Levi wasn't all that thrilled to have him in his space. He should've been grateful and done whatever Levi wanted.

Not moved into his house! He had no doubt in his mind that Levi was going to be furious that Clayton hadn't followed even the simplest of directions. The man had every right to feel that way, too, since he'd never once mentioned a word about Clayton moving into his house, sharing every meal, or spending time with his amazing daughter.

And Heart was amazing. She was beautiful to look at and adorable. As well as kind to small animals. And wayward apprentices.

Clayton felt his cheeks heat in embarrassment. Rightfully so. It seemed he could wax poetic about the woman for hours. From the moment he'd seen her walking up her drive, he'd been practically transfixed. He barely knew her, but his gut screamed that she was the woman for him.

Which, sure as snow falling in July, was impossible.

Not only was she the daughter of a very grumpy and particular man, who kept her shielded from the outside world, but Clayton also had a feeling that Heart Beachy was going to be rich one day. Very rich. Money might not matter in the grand scheme of things, but it would certainly give her many options for her future.

And the plain and simple truth was that Heart could have anyone she wanted—*English* or Amish. Garrett would have called her a catch.

Clayton Glick, a foundling from a children's home with little money and even fewer connections, was most definitely not.

An all-encompassing, unwelcome sense of doom

settled deep in the pit of his stomach as he thought about Levi's reaction to his bold move into the house. It wasn't going to be good.

And, if by chance, he happened to notice the way Clayton couldn't keep his eyes off Heart? Well, that would be even worse. The man already had a reputation for being short-tempered and impatient with fools and slackers. There was no telling how he regarded bold vagabonds encroaching on his space and his daughter.

The only thing Clayton was relatively sure about was that Levi's reaction was going to be full of fire and loathing.

And would end in a swift kick to the curb.

Clayton reckoned he would deserve it, too. He didn't know a lot about family dynamics, but he felt sure that if he was a father and had a daughter like Heart, he would want to keep men like him far away from her.

Walking back out of the barn holding his duffel bag, Clayton slowed his steps as he realized that no matter what his brain might say, his heart told a different story. Honestly, it was as if the two organs were parts of two different people.

His footsteps slowed. Why was he so weak where she was concerned? All Heart had to do was stare at him with those impossibly blue eyes and his whole being reacted.

He knew he wasn't ever going to be able to tell her no.

"You didn't want to," he muttered to himself. "You

can pretend that this move was all her doing, but it had everything to do with you."

Yes, the temptation to be near her was a factor, but living in the barn would've been close enough.

There was a whole other need that he couldn't ignore. The fact was he'd never had a room like that. It was large and well-appointed and comfortable and warm. He wanted it.

Sure, there were other factors at play. Such as the fact that it would likely be snowing harder soon and he didn't fancy having to trudge through it in the dark to take a shower or use the facilities.

Or that he was pretty sure he'd seen a wiry-looking mouse scurry away when he'd climbed the ladder to gather his things. He had no interest in being bitten by a rabid rodent while trying to sleep. He'd been left on his own at a young age, and self-preservation ran deep in him.

By the time he walked to the door, Clayton was as torn up as the shredded paper in Spike's cage.

Though Heart had told him not to knock, he still rapped his hand on the door before opening it.

"Hello?"

Heart walked to the small laundry room. "Hello again."

She was still dressed in a dark blue, long-sleeved dress and black stockings. She still looked as pretty as ever.

Feeling foolish, he said, "I have my things."

"Good!" she called out in a rather merry voice as she returned to the kitchen.

Alone again, he carefully closed the door behind him so Heart wouldn't catch a chill. Then he took a fortifying breath. He was going to do this.

"Clayton, I remember telling you to simply walk inside," she said. Just as if they chatted together all the time.

"I remember." Once again he pulled off his boots. This time, however, he knew where to store them. He arranged them neatly on the boot tray next to the door, trying all the while not to feel like the interloper he was.

After a second's pause he elected to rest his things on the tray, too. If he was minutes from being run out of the house, at least his things would be handy.

Walking into the kitchen, he saw that Heart was at the sink, rinsing off some glasses.

She didn't turn to face him, but obviously knew he was close. "I'm no apprentice, but I have a feeling one needs to learn to follow directions," she teased.

She was being cheeky. No, adorable.

And, because his departure was no doubt imminent, he couldn't resist giving her a bit of attitude, too. "Sorry, but I had only planned on being ordered about by your father."

She laughed. "Point taken. Well, you know where your room is. Go get unpacked and cleaned up. Whatever you need. I put two fresh towels and a handful of washcloths in your bathroom. Supper is at five on the dot."

"You're sure about this?"

"I'm sure." Glancing at him, she frowned. "Where are your things?"

"I left them by the door."

"Go get them and stop worrying."

Turning on his heel, he backtracked, got his backpack and duffel bag, walked through the kitchen, and finally turned down the hall to his room.

When he walked in, he noticed that everything looked the same as when she'd shown it to him, except now there was a pitcher of water and a glass on the bedside table and an additional quilt thrown over the end of the bottom corner of the bed.

Closing the door behind him, he sat down on the comfortable brown chair in the corner, lifted his sock-covered feet to the matching ottoman, and leaned back. It was indeed as comfortable as it looked.

Then, like Goldilocks, he walked to the bed and lay down. It was everything it appeared to be. Comfortable and plush. There were three pillows next to the headboard. Three seemed like an extravagance. For a moment he contemplated actually using all three while he slept—maybe by spreading out like a starfish—until he remembered that Levi hadn't returned home yet.

He got back up and went into the bathroom, felt a lump in his throat when he saw the pile of fluffy white towels Heart had mentioned.

And then, because he was alone and a fool, he pressed the towels to his face. And smelled her. Whatever shampoo or lotion she wore—or maybe it was simply her clean scent—the towels held a slight hint of her. He hastily set them down before walking back to the bedroom.

What to do? He didn't dare unpack. Somehow that action seemed much too presumptuous. But where would he go if he left the room?

Instead, he sat down on the chair and leaned his head back. Closed his eyes.

"*Danke*, *Got*, for bringing me here. Thank you for bringing Levi Beachy into my world. I am grateful for the chance to meet him. Even though I am foolish and unworthy of Heart, thank you for allowing me to meet her. Help me be strong and learn from my mistakes."

Feeling better, he propped up his feet and waited for Levi to return.

He was almost asleep when he heard the man's deep voice in the kitchen.

It seemed the time of reckoning had come.

Chapter 8

"Why are my apprentice's boots next to the door, Heart?"

She'd just sat down at the kitchen table to have a cup of coffee and eat a fortifying monster cookie. The giant cookies were her favorite; they were a combination of peanut butter, chocolate candies, oatmeal, and crushed pretzels. But even the delicious snack wasn't helping to calm her nerves.

Her father wasn't going to be happy with her.

Heart pressed a hand to her chest and braced herself for the conversation that was about to take place. Her father wasn't going to be happy that she'd stepped in to make decisions about Clayton's stay in their home. And "not happy" in Levi Beachy meant that he was going to be scowling and ranting.

She wasn't afraid of her father, but he didn't accept levelheaded reasoning all that well sometimes.

Hearing the clump of his footsteps, Heart gave thanks. At least they could concentrate on boots instead of the fact that she'd told Clayton he could live with them. Thinking that it might be best to look busy, she walked over to the stove.

"Daughter, did you hear me?" *Clomp, clomp,* went his boots.

"I did." Heart stirred the stew a few times.

"And?"

Taking care to turn the knob of the burner off, Heart pulled her shoulders straighter and finally faced her father. As expected, he looked confused and irritated. His arms were folded across his chest. "And we need to talk about that, Daed."

"What is there to talk about? It don't make any sense."

He was practically yelling. Clayton, no doubt, was hearing every word, too. She could only imagine how worried he must be. There was only one thing to do, and that was to pretend all was well, but her father made that impossible.

"You need to lower your voice, Daed."

"Why?"

"Because Clayton will hear you, that's why. You're being rude."

"Rude?" His arms fell to his sides. "The boy is in the barn, daughter. He might be young and spry, but no one's ears are that keen."

"He isn't in the barn, Daed. He's in the guest bedroom." She walked to the table, picked up her mug, and sipped. "Which is why you need to lower your voice."

His brows pinched together. "Say again?"

She lifted her chin. "I told him to stay in the *haus* with us. The barn loft is unlivable."

"You did what?" Before she could answer, he began to pace. "How did this happen?" He shook his head. "*Nee.* More to the point, why?" Again, without giving her a chance to respond, he started down the hall. "Obviously, my apprentice needs to be taught some manners. He took advantage of you in my absence."

She hurried after him and grabbed hold of his arm. Her father was the strongest man she'd ever met. His arms were as solid as tree limbs. Only much bigger. Which was why he barely noticed her attempt to slow him down.

She tugged again, this time using all her strength. "Stop, Daed."

At last, he did. "Not now, Heart."

"*Yes* now. Come on. Stop stomping down the hall and talk to me." She lowered her voice. "Please. This is important."

Her father was no longer moving, but he didn't appear very pleased about stopping to talk. "Child, you not only are named Heart, but you have a good one. I know you mean well, but this man is none of your concern. He's overstepped himself, as well as ignored my rules." Getting riled up again, he waved a hand. "And our agreement. I didn't take on this pup so he could sleep down—"

She pulled on his arm again. "Daed, hush!"

But it was too late. Clayton opened the door. "Your father is right, Heart. I knew it when I went along with your plan. I should've said no. I knew better. Levi, thank you for giving me this opportunity. I'm sure I would've learned a lot."

He was leaving. "Don't go, Clayton. Please just go back in your room."

Those eyes of his warmed. "Although I seem to have a difficult time telling you no, I'm afraid I canna follow your directions this time, Heart. I'm sorry."

She was a grown woman. She could run a whole house—and manage her father. But she still stomped her foot. "Clayton, please. Daed, you are so . . . so bullheaded."

Her father scratched his chin. "Wait a moment. Heart, this was *your* idea?"

"Of course." Since she still had a hand on her father's arm, she squeezed. "I really was trying to tell you about what happened."

At last, her father looked at her. Really looked at her. Then he sighed. "All right. Do you want Clayton to join us or not?"

She answered immediately. "Not. This talk needs to be between the two of us."

Clayton cleared his throat. "So, you do want me to leave now?"

"Not yet, pup. Go to your room," Daed barked.

"Which one?"

"Oh, for the love of Pete." Her father pointed to the guest bedroom. "That one. Go."

Clayton threw up his hands, but did as he was asked. Two seconds later, his bedroom door was shut.

"Come, Daed." She reached for his hand.

To her amazement, he took it. Immediately a feeling that everything was right in the world came over her. Her father's hands were rough and warm and big. When she was little, she'd been sure that all she had to do was hold her father's hand and everything would be right in the world. At least in *her* world.

She smiled.

He noticed. "You haven't gotten your way yet, daughter."

"I know. I was just thinking about holding your hand. I used to think that you could slay dragons, fend off nightmares, and fix anything. Everything was better if I held your hand."

He looked down at their linked hands as they walked to the kitchen. "I used to believe I could," he said in a far softer tone. "Your hand used to be so small in mine. Tiny. I used to fear grasping it too tightly. I was petrified that I would bruise your skin."

"You never did, Daed."

"Ah, child. When did you grow up?"

She shrugged as they sat down at the table. The remains of her cookie were still there. "Do you want a cookie, Daed?"

His lips twitched. "Not yet. Talk to me."

"All right." She wished she was calm enough to pull together all the right words, but there was so much emotion running through her, she knew it wasn't possible. "Sometimes I feel like I've been grown-up for a long time now. Other times it feels like I still have a lot of growing to do."

"There are times when I feel the same way."

"Daed, listen. This all started when Clayton knocked on the door and asked if he could use the toilet."

"What?"

"Father, there's no bathroom in the barn. You know that."

"Jah . . ."

"How did you think he was going to go to the bathroom?"

He scratched his beard. "In the house, of course." Seeming to get his thoughts together, he added, "It's a bit inconvenient, but not that hard to come to the house to use the facilities."

"At night? And shower here and then walk back to the loft?"

"It wouldn't be so bad."

"It would if it was the middle of the night. Plus, it could be snowing out. And dark. And miserable in the barn." She lowered her voice. "You and I both know that there are mice in the barn. No one should have to sleep with mice."

He raised one bushy eyebrow. "You have a rat living in your bedroom. By choice."

"That's different and you know it." When he rubbed a hand over his face, Heart knew she had won. But just to make sure, she said, "Daed, you know this is the right thing to do. I know this Clayton isn't family, but he is going to be working side by side with you. It would be wrong to house him in the barn. Inviting him to use the guest room is what Mamm would want."

He drew in a deep breath. "You had to bring your mother into this?"

"I don't have a choice. She raised me, yes?"

"That, she did." Leaning back in his chair, he suddenly smiled. "The loft is pretty awful."

"It is."

"There were spiderwebs everywhere." He rubbed his beard. "And . . . maybe even a bird's nest."

She couldn't help but smile back at him. "Daed."

"You know what? I probably would've moved him inside sooner or later."

It would've been *later*, but Heart had to give him that. "I know. You're a good man, Daed."

"And as for that rat?"

She tensed. "Yes?"

"I wouldn't mind if he lived in the living room, you know. Mary told me that rats are sociable creatures. He might get bored or lonely sitting by himself in your room all day."

"I reckon you're right. I'll move Spike right now. And . . . will you tell Clayton not to worry about your firing him before he's even started?"

"I'll tell him later. I need to go shower. Supper is coming up soon." He walked away, making her run a hand over her face. Shocked, she realized that she wasn't just her mother's daughter. She'd adopted a few of her father's traits, too.

When she knocked on Clayton's door, he answered immediately. "Yes?"

Looking into his eyes, she felt another small flutter in her chest. He was so handsome. She wished she didn't notice that quite so much.

"Clayton, *mei* father asked me to let you know that there's no need to worry. You're welcome to stay in the house with us."

"Are you sure?"

"I wouldn't lie about that. You don't have to stay in here all the time, either. Feel free to come sit in the living room now, if you'd like."

"You're sure about that, too?"

"Oh, yes. You may keep Spike company. Daed asked that we move the rat into the living room so he won't have to be all alone."

"I see."

Noticing that he looked as if he was attempting to hide his surprise about her father's pronouncement, Heart smiled. "Wonders never cease, ain't so?"

"True, that. Want help with Spike's cage? I could carry it for you."

"*Danke*, Clayton."

Five minutes later, watching him carefully relocate Spike yet again, Heart felt something shift in her chest. She wasn't sure if it was Clayton's presence or her new pet . . . but something had changed.

Something for the better.

Chapter 9

Though he'd always believed that God was good, Clayton hadn't always believed that God was good all the time. At least not for him.

Though he felt guilty for even thinking such a thing, Clayton wasn't going to lie to himself. No matter how kind the staff had been at the children's home, the fact of the matter was that growing up there hadn't been all that wonderful.

His life had been filled with structure, rules, and consequences. Though most people's childhoods were the same, it was different in a home. There were two realities that permeated every waking hour. One was that his parents hadn't wanted him, and the other was that no one else seemed to want him, either.

Every child there was aware of those two things—

and anyone who acted as if it didn't bother him or her? Well, they were liars.

So, being in the home hadn't always been that easy. However, it hadn't been awful, especially for someone like himself who'd been born easygoing and easy to please. He'd done what he was supposed to do and made the best of things.

Not everyone felt the same way, however. Some kids simply couldn't seem to settle into group living. Clayton didn't exactly fault their feelings, but he did feel sorry for them, since anyone who didn't follow the rules had a difficult time of it.

Like his best friend, Angela.

Angela and he had been the same age and had helped each other through school. He'd been good at math and science; she was terrific at spelling, history, and geography. She was bright and had something close to a photographic memory. She also was very sensitive.

As the years passed and it became apparent that they were never going to be adopted, Angela had taken the realization particularly hard.

Clayton swallowed, remembering her last few months at the home. Even though she was smart and could memorize just about anything, Angela had never been a good student. By the time she was fifteen, she'd gotten mouthy and had struggled with their new teacher.

Whether it was that—or the fact that she had no goal in mind for the rest of her life—she'd begun to get depressed. All the girls said that she cried in her sleep and had nightmares at least once a week.

All Clayton had known was that he'd had no idea how to help Angela, and so he'd taken to asking God to look out for her during his nightly prayers.

Then, the day she'd turned sixteen, she'd left.

He'd been concerned. They all had been. He'd even gone to Mr. Weaver and asked him to find her. But the administrator had shaken his head. He'd revealed that while the home had to legally keep children until they were eighteen, they couldn't make them stay once they were sixteen. Angela had wanted to leave.

Clayton had been shocked, but knew better than to question either Angela's wishes or Mr. Weaver's statement. However, it had never felt right. Not for him, and especially not for Angela. He'd asked the Lord dozens of times to look out for her. He hoped He had.

Angela's departure had changed him. He'd stopped focusing on his life in the home and started making plans. One had been to make the social worker take an interest in him and help him get a job at a nearby farm doing chores. And when that farmer had taken him along to the blacksmith one day, Clayton knew he'd found his future.

And now, here he was. Living in Levi Beachy's home and watching Heart make the final preparations on the best meal he'd ever seen.

His current situation was humbling, and he didn't take a bit of it for granted. Though his childhood hadn't been easy, he knew the Lord hadn't forgotten about him. Though his faith hadn't always been the strongest, he felt certain that He really was so good.

He glanced at Spike. The rat was currently resting in

his nest of newspaper and fabric scraps, but his eyes were open. The critter seemed to be taking in the scene with the same feeling of wonder as Clayton.

"We're quite a pair, aren't we, Spike? Neither of us should have it so good, but here we are."

The rat stared at him for a long moment before watching Heart again.

"I don't blame ya. She's a sight, for sure and for certain."

Heart looked his way. "Did you say something?"

"Nee."

She almost smiled. "Wait. Are you speaking to Spike?"

He could lie, but what was the point? "I'm afraid so."

She smiled. "He's going to be a good pet, ain't so? I aim to learn a lot more about fancy rats."

"I'll do the same."

Her expression brightened. "We can go to the library together! We can find some books there."

Realizing that Levi had just joined him, Clayton hesitated.

"Are you gonna answer my daughter?" Levi barked.

"Of course. I was, um, just thinking that I'll likely be so busy with chores for you, I won't have much time for library visits."

"I reckon that will be true. Heart, it's ten after five. Where is supper?"

"On the countertop. The dishes are waiting for the menfolk to take them to the table."

Looking put upon, Levi got to his feet. "Come on,

pup. If I'm feeding ya, you might as well earn your keep. Help me bring out our meal."

"Yes, sir."

He followed Levi into the large kitchen and carefully picked up the casserole dish that Levi had indicated. Levi followed with a dish of glazed carrots. "This looks good," Clayton said as he placed his dish on the table.

"There's more," Levi said. "Go help Heart."

Indeed there was more. A platter of noodles, layered with butter and some kind of herb, and a glass bowl filled with some sort of Jell-O concoction. He picked up both dishes as Heart followed with several serving spoons in her hands.

When the three of them were seated, Levi said, "It is time to give our thanks for the food we are about to receive."

Clayton closed his eyes and gave thanks, not only for the delicious food, but for this moment. Levi and Heart would never know it, but this was the first time he'd ever joined a family for an evening meal. It was something he'd wished for many, many times during his childhood. He could hardly contain his emotions.

When he opened his eyes again, Levi cleared his throat. "Since you are sitting closest to the stew, you may serve." He handed Clayton his bowl.

He grabbed hold of it. "You'd like me to put some in your bowl?"

Levi cast him a dry look. "Tonight, if you please."

"The serving spoon is to the right of it," Heart said.

Clayton spooned one large helping into the dish, glanced at Levi, then added another portion of the stewed chicken. "Will this do?"

"For now."

After passing on Levi's bowl, he took hold of Heart's plate and spooned a far smaller portion into hers. "What do you think? More?"

"I think that is plenty." After taking the dish from him, she placed a serving of carrots on her plate and then passed the bowl of carrots to him. Followed by the noodles. And a roll. Every bit of it was homemade, piping hot, and smelled wonderful.

"This looks very good, Heart. Thank you for making it."

She inclined her head, though her cheeks looked a bit pink.

Clayton waited until both Levi and Heart started eating before spearing a bite-sized piece of chicken on his plate.

"I've never seen a man eat so tentatively," Levi said. "Why, you're acting as if you've never eaten supper before."

"I've eaten supper, but it's never been like this."

Both of his tablemates stared at him in surprise.

"How do you usually eat supper at home?"

He bit his lip. Usually, he tried to wait as long as possible before mentioning his past. Not because he was embarrassed about growing up in the children's home, but because his past either spurred a great many questions or he received looks of pity. He didn't care for either.

But tonight he had no choice. "I grew up in a children's home," he said. "We ate cafeteria style." He put his fork down and motioned with his fingers. "You know, we went through a line. After I left, I've eaten alone, or with the hands in a workroom, or at a restaurant, or my friends and I served ourselves in the kitchen before sitting down. I've never had a meal like this before."

Heart's eyes were wide. If he didn't know any better, he might have even guessed that she was near tears. But that couldn't be true. They were practically strangers.

He jabbed at a glazed carrot and popped it into his mouth. It was as delicious as the stewed chicken.

"When did you leave the home?" Levi asked.

"When I was nineteen. I could've left earlier, but I wasn't sure where to go. The administrator offered to let me stay a little while longer since I was a hard worker. I earned my keep by working on the landscaping and doing odd jobs."

"Where did you eventually go?" Heart asked.

He put his fork down again. "A farmer came to the home, looking for help. I talked to him, and he took me on. I stayed there for four years."

"So . . . you're twenty-three?"

"*Jah*. Though my birthday is just around the corner."

"How did you decide to—"

"Let Clayton eat while it's hot, Heart," Levi interrupted in a gentle tone.

"Of course. I'm sorry, Clayton. Please eat."

They finished most of the meal in near silence. It

was only broken when Levi requested that one of them pass him more food.

"You may have as much as you would like," Heart murmured.

"This is enough. *Danke.*"

She stared at him for a moment, then said, "Daed, do you remember when we had Mamm's two brothers here? Uncle John and Uncle Luke?"

"I do," Levi replied with a slight frown. "They were hard to forget. What made you think of them?"

Heart chuckled. "I was just thinking about how Mamm worked so hard for our guests and they weren't very nice."

Levi grunted. "They were far more than that. They were downright rude."

"You told them so, too."

"I had to. They were running your mother ragged." Levi scowled, as if he'd been personally affronted. "Nothing was good enough. Why, every time Katie sat down, one of them had her running back to the kitchen for something unnecessary."

Clayton glanced at Heart.

She nodded. "*Mei daed* isn't exaggerating. It was shameful."

"I'm sorry." He wasn't sure what he was apologizing for, but what else could he say?

"Eh, no worries." Putting his fork down, Levi's eyes lit up. "I sent them on their way soon enough. The moment that meal was over."

Heart's eyes sparkled. "They were gone within the hour."

"For real?"

"Absolutely. Katie meant the world to me. No one—not even her bossy brothers—was going to be disrespectful to her under my watch."

The story sank into Clayton's bones. He'd never had anyone fight for him like that. Never had anyone care so much about his feelings that they were willing to risk so much, just to make him happy.

But maybe this was merely a Levi sort of reaction. The man was grumpy as a bear.

Or . . . was it more a case of the man having so much love for his wife that he would go to any length to protect her?

"Ah . . . what did Katie say when you kicked out her brothers? I mean, if you don't mind my asking."

"You can ask me whatever you want," Levi replied. "It don't mean I'll answer. In this case, though, I don't mind sharing at all." His expression softened. "*Mei frau* said I was a difficult host, but a mighty good husband."

"She wasn't upset with you."

"*Nee.* They really weren't good to her. I think she was glad they left."

Heart reached out and folded her small hand around her father's meaty one. "We never had any more of her family here again, did we, Daed?"

"Not even for an hour. That was a good thing, too. Katie was from an unfortunate branch of her family."

"How so? Are they sickly?"

"*Nee.* Just rude and ill-mannered."

"And bossy," Heart added. She sighed. "They were even bossy at her funeral."

Levi nodded. "Even though they're Heart's kin, I've never wanted them around."

"Me neither," Heart said.

Feeling that some response was necessary, Clayton said, "I guess that means the home where your wife grew up wasn't all that good." He smiled slightly. "Everything wasn't all roses in the children's home where I grew up, either, but between the two, I know which one I'd pick."

Levi shook his head slowly. "You've got it all wrong, son. You didn't get to pick. None of us do. What happens in one's life ain't always good and it usually isn't easy. But it is what it is. The Lord willed it and that's that."

"I guess that's true." Maybe more than true. Everything did happen for a reason. If he hadn't grown up in the children's home, he never would've gone to the Troyers' farm and become interested in welding and ironworking. If that hadn't happened, no one would've asked Levi if he'd take on an apprentice . . . and Clayton wouldn't have ended up at the table eating this supper.

And something told him that this place and these people were going to be important to him. Maybe he would never be as gifted a blacksmith as Levi was. Maybe he wouldn't be anything close to that.

But he was going to do his best to learn from the man. About work and about life.

Clearing his throat, Clayton said, "I'll do my best never to boss either of you around."

"See that you don't. I'd hate to send you on your way. At least in the middle of winter."

He noticed Heart was looking down at her lap and Levi looked completely serious. And then he noticed Levi winking at Heart.

They were teasing him. Almost as if he already belonged.

At a loss as to how to respond, Clayton returned his attention to his meal.

Chapter 10

Levi liked to think of himself as being a God-fearing man and a realist. For better or worse, it was who he was and his approach to life had served him well through thick and thin. That said, there were occasions when he felt a little dreamy and his mind drifted toward nonsense, when he dwelled on things that had no purpose and didn't do him a lot of good.

He wasn't sure why the Lord decided that he needed those moments, but there had to be a reason. Why else would He continually wake Levi up at the same hour several times a week? At three in the morning, no less!

When Katie had been so sick, Levi had blamed his insomnia on his fretting about her. He'd hated seeing her suffer and hated seeing Heart cry. Because of that, he'd bottled everything up inside and pretended that he was at peace with God's plan. He was sure that was why he hadn't been able to sleep. He'd needed some moments to let go of all that pain.

After Katie passed, his insomnia continued. He barely recalled those empty days and nights. He'd worked tirelessly, unable to come to terms with the fact that his beloved wife wasn't coming back. Or that he now was the sole parent of a grieving daughter and he had no idea about how to make her feel better . . . or even what to do with her.

Now, however, he wasn't sure about why his sleepless nights continued. Did the Lord still believe he was too buttoned-up and needed a private time to deal with all of his emotions?

Or was the reason something far more down-to-earth? Maybe prowling the house at three o'clock had simply become a habit. Maybe it was time for him to stop wondering about the whys and simply accept it.

Lying in his bed, staring at the ceiling, he reckoned that acceptance would likely be the best course of action. He had enough on his mind without trying to analyze his confusing sleep schedule.

Not liking all the unanswered questions, Levi got out of bed and pulled on a hoodie over the old, worn T-shirt that he wore to sleep every night. Katie had once bought him a robe—a voluminous, soft thing. He'd hated it, feeling that it was too heavy, too long, and altogether too much for a man like him. Give him a sweatshirt, flannel pajamas, and a couple of T-shirts and he was good.

He did welcome her introduction of slippers, though.

Every year at Christmas he bought himself a new pair of sheepskin slippers. Looking down at the worn shoes, he reckoned it was time to get some new ones.

Ah, well. For now, he was grateful to have something on his feet. The house was chilly. Even a trip to the kitchen for water was brisk enough for his body to respond. Waking him up even further.

Just as he opened his bedroom door, he heard a noise from the living room. He froze, then remembered that there was now another person in the house.

It was still annoying, but he couldn't say that Heart had been wrong. Katie would've lectured him something awful for even thinking of putting that young man in the barn loft. And then, after he'd apologized to both her and the apprentice, she would've taken Clayton under her wing. She'd always had a soft spot for someone alone in the world. For someone like Clayton.

And him. Though he hadn't been an orphan, Levi had already lost his parents by the time he met Katie. He'd been searching for love and acceptance, and she'd generously gifted him with both.

Thank the good Lord that Heart shared her mother's giving nature and had taken matters into her own hands.

Levi had to admit that the barn was a poor spot to live in. He'd put the bed up in the loft when Katie had been very sick and a nurse had been in the house all the time. He'd found himself not sleeping at night, working in his workshop until he was exhausted, and then passing out on the cot in the loft for a few hours at a time.

He realized now that he probably could've slept through a tornado back then.

Levi paused, unsure whether he wanted to speak to Clayton or not. But in the end he continued down the hall. He was wide-awake, thirsty, and it was his house. That was that.

To his surprise, no one was there. A chill ran through him as his imagination took hold. Had it been Katie's ghost? Or just his overactive imagination?

Just as he took a sip of water, he heard the noise again. And located the source. It was the rat.

Walking toward it, Levi noticed that the tiny creature was watching him closely. Its eyes looked perceptive, as if it actually had thoughts in its brain beyond a need for shelter and food.

Because no one else was around, he walked toward it. "Mary and Heart both told me that you like to stay up at night, too. What do you think about that?"

To his surprise, the rat walked to the gate in his cage. And looked at him expectantly.

The rodent wanted to come out.

Levi took another sip of water before setting the glass down. "Your name is Spike, eh?"

Spike simply stared at him. For a moment Levi was sure the rat was thinking that Levi had a screw loose if he still had to ask about his name.

"Just so you know, it's my daughter who is your caretaker. She's the one who is sweet and kind to small animals. Not me." Though that wasn't exactly true. He surely wasn't the type of man to hurt an animal.

Spike continued to stare expectantly at him.

He wanted to ignore the rat. No, what he wanted was to go back to his comfortable, warm bed, immerse himself in the darkness, and stop thinking. He wanted the gift of oblivion for two full hours that would allow his body and mind to rest.

But he'd sat up far too many of these nights to believe that was going to be possible. He was far too awake. Sleep was not going to return until the sky was dark again.

And the rat did seem like good company. He didn't talk. And . . . hadn't Mary said that the rat liked to be held?

"All right, fine. But if you bite me, don't expect to stay here."

Continuing to stare, Spike twitched his whiskers. Another two seconds passed.

Then Levi decided that handling Spike would do Heart a good service. If the rat became crazed and suddenly snarled or bit him, at least it would be his finger that was injured and not Heart's. Her fingers were too slim and delicate for so much pain.

Bothered by the way he was procrastinating, Levi turned the latch and opened the small gate. "All right, then."

Spike didn't run out. Instead, he took only a few steps forward and poked his long nose out. It was as if he was testing the environment.

Levi gave the rodent his due. "You're right, rat. It's a scary world out here. It's *gut* to be careful. I won't hurt you, though. We might as well be friends, ain't so?"

Spike turned his head and studied Levi. Then, as if he had made up his mind, the rat headed his way.

Next thing Levi knew, he was gently curving his hands around the critter.

The first thing he was aware of was that the rat's fur was soft. That came as something of a surprise. He'd expected it to be rather coarse. Not feel like velvet. He hadn't expected Spike's feet to be cool and soft, either. His claws were sharp, but not overly so. They felt more like the bristles on a broom. Far more delicate than a rose's thorns.

Staring down at the creature, Levi frowned. His hands were so worn and rough, he'd never thought that he would be able to feel something so delicate.

Spike touched one of his fingers with his nose. The slightly damp touch combined with the slight brush of whiskers felt nice.

As if the creature was saying hello.

"Hi, rat. I mean, Spike."

Spike nudged his finger again.

Or perhaps it was simply hungry?

"Sorry, I have nothing for ya at the moment."

Spike twitched his nose, but didn't seem too bothered. Instead, he hopped out of Levi's hand and landed on his thigh.

When he started heading toward his torso, panic set in. "Don't you start crawling all over my lap, rat. My hands might be rough, but I've no mind to have you biting anything down there."

Just as he was about to redirect Spike, the animal

curled up in a ball and . . . snuggled? Levi hardly knew what to think of that. He stared at Spike, his mind spinning as he thought of a dozen reasons to return him to his cage.

But when he gently ran a finger along the animal's fur and noticed how Spike seemed to relax even further, he continued to pet him.

And allowed his mind to drift again. This time his thoughts went toward Mary instead of Katie. And toward Clayton instead of his daughter.

Perhaps surprises were all part of the Lord's plan, just like hardship and beauty. Four years ago, he never would've imagined that he would think about any woman besides Katie. But he was.

Even two years ago, he never would've imagined hiring an apprentice, let alone allowing that man to sleep in his home.

And he surely never would've thought he'd be the type of man to accept a pet rat named Spike into his life.

Or to hold the thing in the middle of the night.

It might be his lack of sleep guiding him again, but something was telling him that in a very odd way everything went together. God had brought Clayton's arrival, Spike's appearance, and the private conversation with Mary Miller all on the same day.

It was fate or kismet or God's will.

He had no idea.

All he did know was that it was all too odd not to notice. He was a lot of things, but he was not the type of man to ignore such signs.

It was time he started living again, and not just in the middle of the night. Maybe he needed to consider living a bit more in the daytime, too. Shake up his schedule and perhaps not work ten hours a day.

Now that he had an apprentice and it was close to Christmas, Levi reckoned it was as good a time as any.

Chapter 11

Mary loved her son, but she wouldn't describe them as close. She wasn't exactly sure why that was. Her mother used to say that a daughter was a daughter for the rest of one's life, but a son was a son until he took a wife.

She supposed that might be true.

In Henry's case, he'd simply been born with a strong independent streak. From the time he was a small boy, he'd never acted like he'd needed her. He simply listened, did what he was supposed to do, and kept to himself. He was a bit closer to Paul. If he was given the choice between spending time with her or his father, his *daed* always won, hands down.

She hadn't faulted Henry for that. Paul had been a

good father to their boy. Patient and kind, he nurtured Henry in all the best ways. He'd also doted on him.

She'd always privately thought maybe a bit too much.

When it became apparent that the Lord wasn't going to bless them with more children, Paul had decided to be Henry's playmate. They'd go fishing after school. Or walking and hiking. Hunting after Thanksgiving. All sorts of male-oriented activities in which she wasn't invited to participate. As the years passed, she and Henry had less and less to talk about—especially when she told him to help with his laundry or wash dishes or go to the store with her.

He'd simply find something else to do. Or worse, ask his father if he wanted to go somewhere together. Paul would always say yes—reminding Mary that since she hadn't been able to have any more children, they only had Henry.

As if somehow Paul's spoiling was a result of her inadequacy. It had been something of a sore subject between them.

When Paul died, it had been devastating for both her and Henry. His sudden death had made each of them reevaluate their lives. For months neither of them had done much; but when the grief subsided, Mary had known that she wanted to help other people, and Henry decided that he had no reason to stick around. Within a year he'd decided not to be baptized and jumped the fence. And then he'd left the house.

Henry's departure had been hard, but she hadn't been

too shocked, either. Honestly, she'd been rather proud of him. Not because he'd chosen not to be baptized, but because Henry had managed to make something of himself. He'd actually moved in with an *English* friend he'd met in middle school. When he'd asked the family if they could help so he could go to high school, they'd taken him in. And then he'd gotten a scholarship to college.

Now Henry was living in Kentucky and had a good job as a manager in a big company. She was proud of him.

She just wished that they were closer. She wished that a lot.

When she'd been able to get a cell phone because she was a woman living alone and she had clients, Mary considered it to be a blessing because it enabled her to easily answer his calls.

Henry did call, too. Every Sunday afternoon he called from his home in Louisville, Kentucky. He lived in the suburbs of the big city with his wife, Amy. Amy had been divorced and was raising two kids on her own when she met Henry. He had fallen in love with her almost immediately, and felt the same way about her children.

They'd married within a year in a small ceremony hosted by Amy's family.

Mary had been the only Amish person present.

Though she never wished Henry was different—the Lord had made her son the way he was—Mary did wish that they were closer. Or, at least, that there was a hope of their becoming closer.

She didn't see that happening, though. Her son loved her, but Mary was in his past. Maybe talking to her reminded him too much of Paul? She didn't know.

All that was going through her mind as she stared at her cell phone and waited for it to ring. Hope sprang eternal. Maybe today was the day Henry would announce that he was coming home for a visit. Or that he wanted her to come down south to be with them for a spell.

At three on the dot the phone rang.

"Hi, Mom."

Sitting in her favorite chair with Virginia and her puppies nearby, she smiled. "Hiya, Henry. How are you?"

"Good. Busy."

She sipped her peppermint tea. "Well, tell me all about everyone. How is Amy? How are Cameron and Shayna?"

"Amy's good. She's started taking painting classes and is playing more tennis."

"Good for her." Mary had never had that kind of extra time, but she couldn't fault Amy for making good use of it. She was a hard worker and did a lot for both Henry and their *kinner*.

"Yeah. She acts like doing something for herself is a big deal, but I told her that she should. She does everything for those kids."

"She sounds like a good mom."

"She is. The kids are good, and I know it's because she keeps such a close eye on them."

"Well, tell me all about them. What's new?"

"Cameron has a girlfriend now. He took her to homecoming."

"Wow, are they serious?"

"I hope not. They're only seventeen. Plus, he's going to be applying to college next year. He's way too young to be serious."

"Ah. Yes." She bit back her words about being seventeen when she'd met Paul. "And Shayna?"

He sighed. "A handful. She never wants to do her chores, Mom. And then Amy ends up doing them for her. Can you believe that?"

"Mmm."

"Plus, she's always on the phone."

"Shayna is only fourteen, *jah?*"

"*Jah.* I mean, yes." He chuckled. "Wow, I haven't thought in Pennsylvania Dutch in months. I wonder what happened?"

"Maybe you've missed your *mamm*," she said before thinking better of it. When he didn't say anything for a moment, Mary winced. She should've watched her tongue. "So m—"

He interrupted her. "Maybe I have missed you."

And just like that, tears formed in her eyes. "Maybe I've missed you, too, Henry."

His voice softened. "When was the last time we saw each other?"

"In June." Six months ago. Henry and his family had come over for lunch on their way to the lake.

"I know we couldn't see you for Thanksgiving because of Amy's family. What about Christmas?"

"I'd enjoy seeing you all at Christmas."

"I'll ask Amy if we could drive up and see you. Maybe we could get together for dinner or something."

She wished he wanted to stay for a day or two, not just a quick meal together before they did something else. Deciding to take what she could get, she tried to sound excited about sharing another meal. "I would like that. I could make all of your favorites. I mean, if you wanted."

"Would you make date nut pudding?"

She now had a lump in her throat. "*Jah*, Henry."

"Next Sunday when I call, I'll let you know."

"Sounds good."

"I guess I'd better go soon."

"Oh. All right." After taking a fortifying sip of tea, she added, "I appreciate you calling."

"Oh, wait. I never even asked how you are. Anything new?"

"Yes, as a matter of fact. Virginia had five puppies."

"That's your golden retriever, right?"

"Yes, son."

"Five puppies? I bet they're adorable."

"They are. They don't have their eyes open yet, but they're already running Virginia ragged. She doesn't even mind when I pick them up."

"Shayna would love them." He chuckled. "So would Cameron."

"All *kinner* love puppies, Henry."

"I guess that's true. Well, have fun with the pups and I'll call you next week."

"All right, Henry. I love you."

"I love you, too, Mamm."

When they hung up, she stared off into space. She felt empty again, but shook it off. There wasn't much she could do about Henry or their relationship, anyway.

Realizing that her tea was turning tepid, she stood up, then started when there was a knock at her door.

"Levi?" she asked as soon as she opened it.

He had on a thick sweater. It was an oatmeal color and looked cozy and warm. His black wool coat was open and he had on a knit beanie instead of a traditional black felt hat. All in all, he looked younger than usual, cozy, and handsome.

And, perhaps, a bit tentative?

He shifted from one foot to the other. "Hiya, Mary. I needed a break, and then I thought maybe you wouldn't mind if I came over to see if you needed some help with the puppies."

"I think they are doing well, but you're welcome to see them. Would you like a cup of hot tea?"

"Sure. It's cold out."

"I bet the walk over here was chilly. You should stay awhile."

Levi didn't seem to need more of an invitation than that. He took off his boots and then padded over to Virginia's whelping box. Virginia was lying on her side, and her five offspring were crowded around her. Each was sound asleep and all of them were in uncomfortable-looking positions, as if each puppy had fallen asleep in midmotion.

When he sat down next to the box, he ran a hand down Virginia's head.

And then one of the pups squeaked and crawled to his hand.

"May I pick it up?"

"Sure."

"And you're positive Virginia won't get mad?"

"If that's the pup with the white spot on its head, she'll probably thank you for taking him for a moment."

"What's wrong with you?" Levi said to the pup.

"He's a handful, that's what he is," she teased as she walked to his side. "Here's your tea."

"Danke." Placing the pup in his lap, he sipped from his drink, then picked up the puppy again. "You look too small to be a handful, pup."

Mary couldn't help but laugh. "That's because your hands are so big. Believe me, he is a bossy guy."

"Does he have a name?"

"Right now, I'm thinking I might call him Trouble."

"No, no. I think you should call him Spot."

"That's not very original," she teased.

"That's true. Neither is Trouble, though." He gently rubbed the puppy again before placing him back with his brothers and sisters. Right away, another puppy crawled to him, anxious to get some attention, too.

"Come here, sweet little girl," he cooed. "Aren't you a beauty?"

Bemused, Mary sipped her tea as she watched Levi cuddle each pup. He was careful and sweet. So sweet, that after watching him for a few moments, Virginia flopped over on her side and closed her eyes, obviously pleased to be given a break.

"I'm glad I came over," he said.

"I'm glad, too."

He stared at her. "You okay? You seem a little blue."

"I'm fine. I just got off the phone with Henry." She'd told Levi about Henry when she was at his house while Katie was so ill. Levi had made no bones about how he felt about her son being so absent from her life.

"Hmph. Is he treating you any better?"

She nodded. "He's never mean."

"I suppose not." He opened his mouth, obviously wanting to share his feelings, but he didn't say anything more.

"Not every child is like Heart, Levi."

"This is true, but I was recently reminded that not every child has a parent. Henry is blessed to have you."

"Danke." Smiling at him, she added, "Anytime you'd like to come over and tell me nice things, please do." She'd meant it as a joke, of course.

But he didn't laugh. Instead, Levi picked up his tea and sipped again. "I just might come over more often, Mary. What do you think about that?"

What to say? "I think that would be nice. If I'm home and not working, then I'd enjoy the company. You are welcome to come over anytime. Anytime at all." Of course, she immediately wished she hadn't sounded quite so eager. "I mean, the puppies are hard to ignore, right?"

"Virginia's pups are adorable. That is true." Levi picked up another pup and held it in his lap. Sipped his tea. "But maybe they're not the only reason I might feel like visiting."

Mary knew what he was hinting at. It made her feel warm inside, as if she wasn't just a widow who worked hard and had a son who'd grown up and grown out of her life.

Levi made her feel as if she was something more. It felt good. Really good.

But because she wasn't certain about how to respond, Mary took the coward's way out. She picked up another pup and plopped it on her lap.

And allowed herself to enjoy the fact that she wasn't sitting alone.

Chapter 12

It was Wednesday, and Clayton's third day of working for Levi. So far, things were going fairly well.

The forge was running smoothly and operating at the appropriate temperature. It had taken some time to learn how to regulate the flames, but he was learning.

At first, Clayton had been at a loss when he'd learned that Levi used propane instead of coal to fuel the fire, but after Levi told him his reasons—all to do with being able to regulate the temperature more accurately— the use of propane made sense.

There was also the added benefit of being able to start the fire much more efficiently. And, it seemed, to extinguish it as well.

After they'd worked on the basics of running the

forge, they'd moved to the anvil, the smithy's work-table. Though Clayton had made horseshoes before, his former teacher was a mere amateur in comparison to his new one. Levi not only made working with heavy, hot steel look easy, he was able to sense the temperature of the metal without so much as looking at the thermostat.

It was impressive.

But not as impressive—at least not to Clayton—as his teacher's patience with him. Clayton never would've imagined Levi to be as quiet and soft-spoken as he was with him.

Even when he was making mistakes.

And he'd sure made quite a few of them. Clayton was surprised he hadn't burned either Levi, himself, or the barn during their first morning together. He'd been so nervous around the man that he'd kept messing up or second-guessing himself. Following every mistake, he would tense up, mentally preparing to be kicked off the property.

Finally, after Levi had given him a tall glass of water, sat him down, and assured him that he was not going to fire him because he wasn't perfect, Clayton relaxed.

Kind of.

But now that they were in the middle of their third day, Clayton felt as if he was finally finding his way. Perhaps it was because the two of them had started to develop a routine.

The first thing in the morning, Clayton helped with

simple farm chores, like gathering eggs, mucking out
the horse's stall, and shoveling the walkway from the
house to the barn.

After consuming every bite of Heart's delicious
breakfast, Clayton would then organize Levi's day and
write everything neatly on a big board in the work-
space. Then he would light the forge and help Levi as
much as he could.

So far, no matter how busy they were, Levi always
made time to let Clayton practice. It turned out that he
was a very good teacher. His directions were clear and
precise and calm.

"*Jah.* There you go," Levi said. He was standing a
few feet away. Close enough to give Clayton a hand if
need be, but far enough to allow him to feel that he was
crafting the horseshoe on his own. "How does that
feel?"

Clayton knew what Levi was asking. He was referring to the way the metal felt on the work surface. The
way he was able to use his tongs to form the shoe into
the perfect shape. "Better," he said honestly. "Much
better."

Levi nodded. "I'm pleased. You've earned yourself a
break. Put the tongs down and hang up your apron. Go
into the house and get a good drink of water." He
winked. "See if Heart needs some help, or maybe she
has decided to take pity on us and made us cookies,
too."

"Do you think there's a chance?" Heart had made
her father's favorite cereal bars soon after he'd arrived.

When her father had eaten almost the entire batch in one sitting, she'd looked a little put out.

"There's always a chance, pup." He waved a hand, shooing him out of the workshop. "Go on now. Get some fresh air."

"I don't mind working hard." He didn't want Levi to think that he was lazy or weak.

"Pup, it's already past three. We've been at it for almost four hours."

"I can't believe it."

"Your muscles can. I will tell you that. They're going to be screaming at ya all night if you ain't careful."

Clayton feared he was right. He'd been so sore after the first morning they'd worked together, he'd barely been able to roll over in his bed.

There was a reason most blacksmiths were burly men. Working in the forge with heavy metals and heavy tools created more muscles than a day at the gym. "I thought I was in shape, but obviously not."

"Don't be so hard on yourself. You're doing fine."

"Not hardly."

"No one is born knowing how to work with hot metal, Clayton." He shot him a knowing look. "Don't kid yourself. If I wasn't pleased with ya or didn't think you had promise, I'd let you know."

Levi thought he had promise. That compliment meant so much, Clayton's mouth was dry. "I . . . I'm relieved to hear that."

"Don't worry so much. You need a break and I want

to work on a commission for a couple of hours, so go
on," Levi urged.

"Okay, sir."

"Danke." Levi spared Clayton a quick nod before
walking to the back of his shop and moving over a
wheeled cart with what looked like the beginnings of a
horse on it.

Even though it wasn't even halfway done, the fine
workmanship was easy to see. It was humbling to witness what Levi was able to create with seeming ease
while it took Clayton ages to form a decent horseshoe.

He would've liked to have stayed to observe, but
Levi had already made it known that wasn't an option.
He liked to work alone. Period.

After removing his gloves and apron, Clayton reached
for his coat and walked outside.

The snow had continued and was falling still. Easily,
four or five inches of powder had fallen since they'd
stopped for lunch. Though he'd quickly cleared it before returning to the forge, the path that led from the
house to the barn was filling, as were the steps leading
to the front and back doors. Heart shouldn't have to
shovel any of that.

Deciding that it wouldn't do any harm to shovel the
path now and the steps later, Clayton retrieved the im-
plement and neatly cleared the walk. Then, after he put
the shovel away, he strode to the house.

Walking down the now-cleared path, he made a list
of things to do. Water, perhaps get something to eat.
Shovel. Help Heart for a spell, then go back out and get
to work. It was a full day, and a busy and fulfilling one.

After removing his boots and washing his hands well in the stationary tub at the back door, he padded into the kitchen, hoping to find Heart.

After helping himself to a large glass of water, he decided to look for her in one of the bedrooms, but drew up short when he found her sitting on a chair in the living room with Spike. The rat was in one of her hands, eating a grape. Her expression was so at peace, he hated to disturb her.

She looked up when he approached.

"Clayton. Hello." As always, her voice was smooth and melodic.

"Hi. Your father sent me in for water and to help you for a spell."

"Hmm."

"I'm going to shovel the snow off the steps, but wanted to check on you first. Is everything okay?"

She smiled as she handed Spike another grape. "*Jah*. You caught me resting a bit myself. I thought I should get to know our pet a little better."

Unable to help himself, Clayton sat down on a chair across from Heart. He told himself that she'd probably like a little bit of company, but the truth was that he was the one who needed her. Her sweet manner was everything her father's was not. Everything he'd never had. "I reckon feeding him grapes is a good start," he said.

"It seems to be working. At first, I was afraid that he might be skittish with me, since I'm a stranger, but he didn't try to evade my hand at all when I reached inside to take him out."

"He would be foolish to bite the hand that feeds him, ain't so?"

She chuckled. "Indeed." After watching the rat finish his grape, she ran a finger down his side.

Clayton could have sworn that the little thing leaned into her touch. Spike liked her.

"I think you made the right decision to bring him home."

"I couldn't allow someone to let Spike loose in the wild. Or worse, kill him. That isn't right."

"No, it isn't."

She patted the rat again and then stood up. "I bet you're hungry. Would you care for a snack?"

"I'm hungry, but I can get myself something in a little while—as well as clean it up. You don't need to fuss over me."

Heart stood up. Instead of depositing Spike in his container, she allowed him to stay on her chair. "I never asked, did you sleep all right last night, Clayton?"

His bed was very comfortable. Just like the previous nights, he'd fallen asleep practically the second he'd finished his prayers. "Very much so. Why?"

"It was the strangest thing. When I woke up and checked Spike's cage, I noticed that his water bottle was filled. I thought maybe you had done it in the middle of the night."

"It wasn't me. I slept the whole night through."

"I guess it was my father."

There was no other option, of course. But he still found it hard to believe. "I wouldn't have thought your father would be the sort to tend to a rat."

"You'd be surprised." She chuckled at Spike, who had deftly climbed to the chair's armrest. Clayton was afraid he was about to start chewing the upholstery, but instead the animal seemed content to merely observe the two of them from his perch.

Looking as if she wanted to make sure the rat wasn't going to fall off the chair, Heart added, "*Mei daed* is gruff and doesn't think about making a mess on my kitchen floor. But he does have a good heart." She smiled at him. "At least for animals and children."

"I'm glad."

A knowing gleam entered her eyes. "Is my father giving you a hard time, Clayton? I promise, you don't need to guard your tongue with me. I've lived with him a long time and know that sometimes he can be more than a little difficult to please."

Thinking that Levi was an exacting boss, yet still took the time to explain things well, Clayton shook his head. "I have no complaints."

"Truly?"

"Truly." It was the truth, too. Though he would never complain to Levi's daughter about him. He, like Spike, was in no hurry to bite the hand that fed him.

Standing up, he looked around the room. "Now, Miss Beachy, what may I help you do around here before shoveling the steps?"

"Nothing. I've got everything well in hand."

"I mean it. Not only did your father ask me to help ya, I want to be useful."

"Clayton, I promise that I'm used to doing everything."

"That isn't exactly a good thing." Pointing to the broom that he'd just noticed propped against the wall, he said, "How about I sweep the floors?"

"*Nee.* The floors are fine."

He looked around. Tried to think of something else that would help without getting in the way. "Dust?"

"Dust?" She chuckled. "Oh, Clayton. You aren't going to give up, are you?"

"Nope."

"I guess that means I'm going to have to do something with ya." Playfully she placed a hand on her hip. "I wonder what?"

A handful of activities ran through his head—beginning with simply sitting next to him and ending with her in his arms. Not a bit of it was appropriate.

All he seemed to be able to do was stand there and wait. And hope that she didn't send him away.

Chapter 13

Clayton shifted his weight as he forced himself to wait for Heart to suggest something for him to do. That didn't stop his mind from spinning, however. A dozen ideas came to mind—all of them rather ridiculous. Though he'd learned, growing up, to make beds and clean bathrooms, most of his chores had been outside. He would be next to no help with laundry or in the kitchen.

At last, she answered, though she looked hesitant. "I thought of something, but it seems like an imposition."

"It won't be."

Her blue eyes sparkled. "Clayton, you don't even know what I'm going to ask!"

He knew that he owed her his bed and room. He also knew that he had enough of a crush on her that he wouldn't be able to deny her much of anything. No matter what she asked him to do.

Of course, he couldn't say such a thing. "You do a lot for me, ain't so?"

"Jah."

Some of the mirth he'd spied in her expression had faded a bit. It almost looked as if she was disappointed by his comment. Eager to make amends, he said, "So, what may I do?"

"Well, you could help me bring up some boxes from the basement, I suppose. If you're sure you don't mind?"

"I'm sure." This time he was the one who couldn't resist teasing her a bit. "Heart, it's just a chore, ain't so?"

She seemed to come to a decision. "All right." She scooped up Spike, who'd fallen asleep, and gently deposited him in his cage, then smoothed the skirts of her dress. "Let's go downstairs, then."

She went down the hall and opened the door at the very end of it. Attached to the wall was a plastic compartment. A battery-powered flashlight was stored inside. Heart pulled it out, turned it on, and walked down the wooden steps.

He followed on her heels. As expected, the basement was dark and chilly. It was a blessing that the flashlight was powerful enough to cut a wide beam of light in front of them.

"The storage room is over here." She pointed to a space off to the side filled with several dozen boxes and large plastic tubs.

There didn't seem to be any rhyme or reason to the

way they were organized or stacked. That surprised him. Levi's workshop was meticulous and the house seemed well organized, too.

"What are we looking for?"

"Christmas decorations." Stepping into the mess, Heart shoved one box off a crate. "They're someplace around here. At least I think so."

"You decorate for Christmas?"

"Jah." Still holding the flashlight in one hand, she attempted to move another box with one hand. Not only was it large, but it also looked very heavy. It teetered on the corner.

He rushed forward and grabbed the box before it crashed to the floor. Or on her foot. "Just point and I'll move, okay?"

"Hmm?" She crouched down to read a label. "Why?"

"Because they look heavy, and you could get hurt." Wasn't the answer obvious? He had at least seventy pounds on her. He felt like rolling his eyes.

"I'll be fine. I haven't gotten injured down here yet."

He had a feeling that happy statement had more to do with the grace of God than anything else. "Heart, I'm here now. Plus, your father asked me to help you. If you move boxes around without me, it's going to upset him." And it would upset Clayton, too. He wanted to be there for her.

She finally turned to look at him. A chunk of her hair had escaped its confines and had fallen against her cheek. Even in the dim light he was struck by the color of her eyes and the sheen on her golden hair.

"Fine," she said, pulling him back to the present. "I

think the Christmas decorations are in that red plastic crate at the bottom of the stack."

"All right."

"There might be some in one of the cardboard boxes, too."

There were only about thirteen of them. "Which ones? Any idea?"

"*Nee.* But they'll be easy to find. Each has a label on its side." She nibbled her lip. "Or maybe the top."

"You really have no idea?"

"It's been a long time since I've brought the boxes upstairs."

"What does the label say?"

"Christmas, of course."

"All right, then. You move to the side and I'll take care of this for you."

Heart sighed, but did as he asked. After moving around several boxes, each covered with dust, he shook his head in exasperation. The whole arrangement looked like it was just waiting for a strong wind—or an excited Labrador—to blow all the wobbling towers down. While it was no trouble for him to move them around, he hated the thought of Heart doing the chore by herself with only a flashlight's beam to aid her progress.

"What is in all of these boxes?" he asked as he lifted another one and set it on the floor.

"All sorts of things. Extra jars for summer canning. Baby clothes. Old toys and books. Items for outside in the summer." She frowned. "Come to think of it, I'm not really sure."

Noticing that the cardboard on the box he'd just lifted

was in danger of disintegrating, he frowned. "Your family likes to save things."

"I guess. Doesn't everyone's?"

"I have no idea." He'd meant for it to come across as a joke. However, the moment the words left his mouth, he realized that Heart was taking his words seriously. "Sorry."

"Nee." She pressed one delicate-looking hand to her mouth. "I'm the one who is sorry. I shouldn't have said what I did. It was rude of me to mention."

"It wasn't." When she continued to look stricken, he stepped over an old blanket to reach her side. "Heart, I'm not going to tell you that I loved every moment of living in the children's home, but I'm sure not going to tell you that it was awful. I didn't know any different. Plus, I reckon I'm a little rough around the edges, especially when it comes to minding my tongue. I spent lots of time with other boys and girls my age. I got a bit too used to saying whatever was on my mind."

"That doesn't make me feel any better. Or any less sorry for you."

"I don't want your pity. But listen. I also don't want you to think that I'm sensitive about my childhood. I'm not. I don't mind talking about it. I'd have a worse time if I thought it stood between us." When she still looked torn, he spoke faster. "I'm serious. I might be here for a while. I mean, if your father doesn't fire me. I don't want things to be awkward between us."

She released a ragged sigh. "Fine."

"Promise?" He bent his knees a bit so he could look her in the eye.

"I promise."

He straightened. "*Gut.* Now let's get your Christmas decorations before we discover that this mess is infested with mice."

"It is not."

He would be surprised if she was right. He hadn't noticed any mousetraps and the space had obviously been neglected for some time. It was a mouse mecca. "You know what? This is a hodgepodge of boxes. I'll start working down here in the evenings and organize it."

"You'll do no such thing! I can do it."

Instead of replying with the obvious—that it was too much of a job for a slight girl—he shrugged. "That's what I'm here for." After lifting another three boxes and moving them to one side, he spied the label: CHRISTMAS. "Success! It looks like all three of these boxes are labeled for Christmas. Which ones do you want brought upstairs? Or do you want all of them?" If she wanted all of them, half of the dining room was going to be filled with boxes.

"*Nee*, not all. Just the red plastic crate. And . . . that cardboard box right next to it."

"Gotcha."

Clayton had to move a couple more boxes around, but he was able at last to lift the red tub and carry it upstairs as Heart beamed the light so he could see his way.

"Where would you like it?"

"The living room."

"Give me the flashlight and I'll go get the carton."

"Could you get the others as well?"

He hid a smile. *"Jah."*

"Wait! You're gonna need my help getting up and down."

He reached for the flashlight. "I've got it. It's cold down there." He headed down before she had time to argue. Walking down, he wondered how she'd brought up everything in the past. Had she somehow moved all the boxes by herself? She must have, but he had a hard time imagining Levi standing by while she did that.

Figuring it didn't matter—for there was nothing he could do about the past—he picked up the box, which was much lighter than the red tub, positioned the flashlight so the beam lit his way, and climbed the stairs yet again.

Heart was sitting on the floor next to the red tub. The lid was open and she had a red tablecloth on her lap. Someone had embroidered an intricate design around the edges with black floss. She smiled at him. "Isn't this pretty? *Mei mamm* stitched it."

"It is pretty. Do you remember her making that?"

"Oh, *nee*. She stitched it when she was little. Mamm's *daed* was Amish, but her mother grew up *English*. Mamm told me that she learned to do a few things like embroidery from her *mamm*. I guess they did a lot of things together during the long winter months when she was small."

"I'm glad you have them."

"Me too." Running a finger along the fabric, she glanced at him. "Hey, Clayton?"

"Hmm?"

"Thank you for helping me. I appreciate it."

"Like I said, I'm happy to help you with anything you need."

"Because my father asked you to."

Agreeing with that statement was the right thing to say. The smart thing. But he didn't seem to be smart at all where she was concerned. "I respect your father, but that's not the only reason why I helped." He lowered his voice. "It's because I want to help you. Very much."

Her eyes widened and her lips parted slightly. Practically begging for him to lean in.

He turned before he did something stupid like kiss her. "I'll bring up the rest of the boxes," he muttered before hurrying down the stairs.

Twenty minutes later, just after he'd carried the last of the boxes up and had given in to Heart's plea to sit on the floor and keep her company, the back door opened.

Clayton barely had time to turn before Levi strode in. When he saw Heart on the floor, he frowned, but his expression blanched when he saw what was in her hands.

"What are you doing with that?"

Her happy smile dimmed. "Clayton brought it upstairs for me."

He scowled at Clayton. "I told you to do some chores for my daughter. What made you think that I wanted you inspecting my basement?"

Clayton flinched. The man's scathing tone took him off guard, but he knew Levi well enough by now to realize that the other man expected Clayton to stand up for himself. "I wasna inspecting anything."

"I asked Clayton to bring up the decorations, Daed," Heart blurted.

"We don't need them. Especially not that." He was eyeing the pretty cloth as if it could suddenly come alive and attack them.

"It is Mamm's special tablecloth. I want to put it on the table until Christmas."

Levi scowled. "It ain't Plain."

Heart flinched at his tone. "I know that. But Mamm liked it, anyway. You used to like it, too, Daed. Don't you remember?" Her voice softened. "You used to tell Mamm the bright red color made you think of cardinals in the trees."

Pain flickered in his eyes before he scowled at her. "Having that tablecloth out won't make your *mamm* come back, Heart. She's gone."

Clayton was so shocked by the venomous tone in Levi's voice, he could hardly speak. That paralysis only lasted a scant few seconds, though. On its heels came an anger that could've been fueled by the hot flames of Levi's forge.

"She's not gone, Daed. She's dead." When Heart stood up, the tablecloth discarded at her feet, her expression was so ravaged, she looked like a shadow of herself. Grief and anger had doused her spark.

Clayton stepped forward. What he could do for her, he didn't know, but he wanted to do something to ease her pain. He stopped himself in time. He hadn't even been on the Beachys' property a whole week. Neither Heart nor Levi would appreciate his stepping in where he didn't belong.

Heart walked past them both on her way to the mudroom. Clayton heard her sniff as she put on her cloak and boots before the door opened. Seconds later, it slammed shut.

Levi winced.

The weather had turned colder, and it was still snowing. Though it wasn't up to him to look out for her, Clayton wondered if she'd taken the time to put on a bonnet and gloves. He turned to the window, looking for a sign of her. He saw nothing. She was already out of sight.

Disappointed, he scanned the area as worry for her safety set in again. It was only half past four, but already the sun had begun to make its descent. Within the hour it would be dark. And that knot of worry he couldn't seem to discard when it came to Heart Beachy tightened yet again. He turned to face Levi. "Where do you think she'll go?" he asked.

Levi was standing motionless. His cheeks were stained red. "I don't know," he said after several seconds passed.

"It's going to be dark soon."

"I know that."

"Should I go after her?"

"Nee." He hung his head before seeming to collect himself. "My daughter doesn't leave like this often, but she's done it before. She, ah, has a bit of a temper. Heart usually walks it off and returns when she's calm." He

waved a hand. "I can be difficult from time to time. I, ah, can't exactly blame her for needing some space."

Clayton picked up the tablecloth from the floor. Remembering the way she'd smoothed the material so lovingly, he folded it into a neat rectangle. He could feel Levi watching him, but didn't meet his gaze. That was probably for the best, he reckoned. His feelings toward his mentor weren't very kind just now, and his feelings for the girl he hardly knew were confusing.

When he bent down to put the cloth back in the red tub, Levi stopped him.

"*Nee.* Set it on the dining-room table, Clayton. Heart was right. Her mother liked that tablecloth. She has every right to put it out if she chooses to."

He set it down on the table. "Levi, what would you like me to do now?"

"Eat something, if you're hungry. Then I want you to go to the workshop and straighten everything. Check the fire, too. It should be almost out. But if it's not . . ."

"If it's not, I'll deal with it."

"*Gut.*" Looking as if he was heading to a funeral, Levi glanced out the window. "I'm going out to find her." Walking into the mudroom, he called out, "I'll be back after a while."

"Sir, what should I do if Heart returns? Do you want me to try to find you?"

"*Nee.* No reason for all of us to be out gallivanting around and searching for each other. If Heart returns, make sure she stays put and, ah, make sure she gets something warm to drink."

"Yes, sir."

"And tell her that I'll be home soon."

"Are you sure you don't want me to go, too?"

"I'm sure." Looking more confident, he added, "I'm going to find her. I have an idea about where to look."

He walked out the door, leaving Clayton alone.

"Tsssk. Tsssk."

Startled, he saw that Spike was standing at the door of his cage and glaring at him. When he squeeked again, it sounded angry. Clayton was sure Spike was scolding him.

"I agree, Spike. I should've gone after her. No matter the weather, she shouldn't be alone right now."

Chapter 14

The changing of her name aside, Heart liked to think that she was fairly easygoing. And a rather adaptable person. Small changes didn't bother her too much. For the most part, she tried to be good and helpful. She often tried to be brave.

Most of all, Heart tried not to let regrets cloud her life or her spirit. Her mother's favorite scripture verse was from Isaiah: *Arise, shine; for your light has come. And the glory of the Lord has risen upon you.* She had quoted it often.

Heart had taken her mother's words to heart. Mamm had often said that few things could change just by one's will or a prayer in the middle of the night. Not likes or dislikes. Not the weather. Not someone's reaction to her.

And certainly not life or death.

Some of those lessons had been hard for Heart to accept, especially about life and death. Heart had certainly wished for things to be different a time or two. She'd prayed and prayed for her mother to get better instead of worse, for her father to suddenly become talkative and perceptive.

Even for Billy Weaver to decide that she was worth courting—though he was afraid of her father.

None of those things had ever happened. Not her mother's return to health or Billy Weaver's attentions.

Her mother would've been disappointed to realize that both her daughter and her husband still missed her so much. She would've reminded Heart that it was a waste of energy and time to wish for things to be different. What was happening at the moment was reality, and it did no one any good to wish for things to be different.

When her mother had gotten sick so suddenly, and then grew weaker with each passing day, Heart had resented that attitude. But as in most things her wise mother had been right. It was better to accept hard things than to pretend they were different. Trite words, perhaps. But so very true.

It would've been nice if she'd accepted her mother's advice a hundred percent. Unfortunately, she didn't. Not completely.

Which was why she was in the predicament that she was in—tromping down the narrow lane connecting her farm to their neighbors' homesteads. While it was snowing.

And almost suppertime.

Heart knew she should turn back, but she just wasn't ready. Continuing on, she could see the faint glow of the setting sun through the snowflakes. It was rather pretty. Before long, the sun would disappear from the horizon. It would be dark, and she had no flashlight.

The snow had lessened a bit. The heavy flakes had become lighter, more delicate. Fluttery, wispy, dancing things, dampening her cheeks and eyelashes. Decorating the dark wool of her cloak with beauty for a split second before dissolving into the fabric. The sight made her sad. She was starting to feel that so much of life's happiness was fleeting.

Like her beloved mother.

Or those sweet moments with Clayton. He'd made her feel special, as if she was worth his time. Even if spending time with her might mean incurring Levi Beachy's wrath.

But then her father had come in and ruined everything.

"Heart?" Mary called out. "That's you, isn't it?"

Mary was out with her dog. Heart was surprised Mary recognized her, since she had on her black bonnet and cloak, which made her look like every other Amish woman from a distance. "*Jah.* It's me."

"What are you doing out this time of day?"

It took her a moment to realize that she was close to Mary's house. She must have walked in a wide circle. "I needed to go for a walk."

"Well, it's too late for a young woman such as yourself to be outside on her own. Plus, it's getting colder.

And snowing." Hurrying to her side, Mary wrapped an arm around Heart's shoulders. "Uh-oh. Something must have happened. Are you okay?"

"I'm fine. I just needed a bit of space."

Concern filled Mary's brown eyes. "I see. Well, dear, I think you've been able to get that. How about I walk you home now?"

Mary was so kind. Warm and kind and likable.

In this case, she was also very wise. No doubt her father was worried sick about her. For that matter, even Clayton would likely be watching the yard for her approach. She was causing undue worry for them.

Taking Mary's suggestion was the right thing to do.

Unfortunately, foolish pride prevented her from accepting the offer. She jutted her chin up. "I don't need a sitter, Mary. I'll head back soon. Home isn't far."

"It isn't far, but it's late." She squeezed Heart's shoulder again before releasing it. "You know what, I'm simply going to take you back."

"Mary, I'm not ready."

"Nope. No more arguments. Walk with me to the house so I can put Virginia back inside, and then we'll head to your place."

Mary's voice was firm. "All right."

"Thank you for not arguing any further."

It took less than ten minutes to get to Mary's house. Once they arrived at the back door, Virginia barked and wagged her tail.

Heart rubbed the retriever's soft ears. "I think she's ready to get back to her pups."

"I'd say so," Mary said with a fond look at her dog.

"I've heard mothers need a break from time to time, but they're always happy to return to their babies. Do you want to come in to see the puppies?"

"I would if it wasn't so late." Good sense was beginning to return. "I just realized that I should have thought about my father. He's likely wondering what's happened to me."

"I fear you are right. I imagine Levi is worried sick." She bent down to unhook Virginia's lead. "You stay here then. Don't leave. I'm going to put her inside and then I'll be back out." After a couple of steps she looked around at Heart. "You will wait for me, yes?"

"Yes."

Heart didn't want Mary's company, but couldn't bring herself to knowingly ignore the woman's wishes.

Sure enough, she was soon back out. Somehow she'd managed to pour hot chocolate into two thermal cups. "Here you go."

"How did you manage to prepare this so quickly?"

"I already had the water heated and in a thermal carafe. It's that kind of day, don't you think?"

"I think so." She sipped the drink. "Is it your own mix?"

"It is. Nothing wrong with Swiss Miss, but I like this mix, too."

"I do as well."

After taking another fortifying sip, Heart felt her body ease.

"What happened, Heart?" Mary asked in her kind way as they began to walk. "Why did you take off?"

"I don't know. I've been arguing with my father a lot

lately. First about letting Clayton stay in the house and then today it was about Mamm's Christmas tablecloth."

She frowned. "Who's Clayton?"

"He's my father's new apprentice. Daed was going to make him live in the barn loft, but that wasn't right." She glanced at Mary to see that she understood. "It's dirty and you have to climb a ladder to get to the room and there's no bathroom out there."

"That does sound rather dreadful. Let me guess . . . there's also no heat?"

"Not a bit of it." Getting worked up again, she raised her voice. "Clayton is really nice, too. And he stares at Daed like he's amazing, which makes it even more awkward."

"For you or Clayton?"

Heart knew Mary was teasing, but she didn't care. "For him! He has to do chores all day and listen to *mei daed* bark and fuss . . . and then we were going to make him sleep in a cold barn without a toilet or a shower? It wasn't right."

"I would've done the same thing as you."

Feeling a little foolish for the speech, Heart chuckled. "Sorry. I guess I'm still a bit irritated about it. Anyway, I moved him into the guest room without my father's permission."

"Oh, dear. What happened?"

"Daed fussed, but agreed that it was silly to have an empty guest room sit vacant, while Clayton lived with the mice in the loft."

"That makes perfect sense to me. So your decision was a good thing."

"Jah." She sipped from the cocoa again. "This afternoon I asked Clayton to help me get out some of my mother's Christmas decorations. When I put out Mamm's tablecloth, Daed got angry, and then I did, too."

"I'm sorry, Heart."

"I am, too. Mary, I don't know what's wrong with me. Some years I don't even get out Mamm's things. Christmas Day just looks like any other day of the year. I usually feel agreeable." She swallowed hard, hoping to ease the lump that had just formed in her throat.

"Ach, Heart. It's okay."

"Is it?" She bit her lip, weighing the pros and cons of divulging even more. Maybe she shouldn't share so much, but it felt good. She was tired of holding everything in. And Mary . . . Well, Mary had been with them during their worst days when her mother passed. She was with sick and dying people all the time. If anyone had the patience and forbearance to deal with imperfect people, it had to be her.

Taking a deep breath, Heart plunged forward. "Mary, all I want to do is get my way sometimes. Even though I know it upsets my father, I'm tired of always doing what he wants." She waved a hand. "I'm even tired of sweeping the kitchen floor every time he tracks mud and dirt on it!"

"You are not being unreasonable. Anyone would be tired of that, dear."

Heart figured Mary was right, but that wasn't how it was at her house. It hadn't ever been. "It's like my entire being is tired of being good." She released a deep breath. There. She'd said it. She'd spoken the whole awful truth.

Mary didn't reply immediately. Instead, all Heart could hear was the wind blowing the tree limbs in the woods to her right. The faint complaint of a squirrel. The distant crunch of twigs. The sounds were as familiar as her complaints, and as dear to her as the lines around her father's eyes. She loved her *daed*. She'd always adored him. Why did his eccentricities bother her all of a sudden?

"It sounds to me like you're growing up."

"Mary, I'm in my midtwenties. I've been grown up for quite a while. But . . . do you think that's it?"

"I do. This is only my opinion, but it seems to me that you've been so intent on helping your father and taking your mother's place that you forgot to focus on yourself. Maybe the Lord decided to step in and help you do that."

"If He did, I wish He'd given me some warning. This isn't easy."

Mary laughed softly. "I don't think He finds that a bad thing."

"I reckon you're right."

"You know, being a good person doesn't mean one always caves in. There's nothing wrong with having opinions, Heart. Nothing wrong with that at all."

"Maybe. I'd like to think that I haven't completely lost my . . . Oh, no. There's Daed."

He was maybe fifty feet away. Still quite far off, but no one else looked like him. Her father was so big and he walked with such confidence, even his silhouette was unmistakable.

She lifted her cup, hoping for a fortifying sip of hot chocolate, but there was none left. "Great," she muttered.

"Don't be afraid. You know your father is only worried."

"I'm not afraid of him." When Mary still looked concerned, Heart said, "Well, I'm a little afraid of what he's going to say, but he would never hurt me, Mary. He's my *daed*."

"Yes. Of course. I didn't think he would."

Their pace slowed as the distance between them lessened. "I suppose I should let him say what he wants to say. He looks pretty mad."

"Heart, I really think he's been worried about you. Let's think about that."

"Okay."

Her father's voice boomed over the expanse between them, likely scaring all the animals and birds in the area. "Heart!"

"He sounds mad, too."

"I'm afraid he does, dear."

Heart wasn't sure if the strain in Mary's voice was because she was worried about Heart, dreading the full force of Levi Beachy's wrath . . . or maybe slightly amused that she was caught in the middle of their family drama.

"Heart!"

"I'm right here, Daed! Obviously."

Mary stiffened beside her. And her father's irritated glower deepened. Yep, there she went again. Saying things that she used to never even think.

Something was very wrong with her.

Honestly, it didn't make a lick of sense.

Chapter 15

Standing in the snow, just a couple of yards from her house, Mary felt completely dismayed. How in the world had she gotten in the middle of a disagreement between the Beachys?

As she watched Levi stride toward Heart, his expression even darker and more foreboding than usual, Mary didn't know whether to stand in front of Heart or simply get out of the way.

Surprisingly, the usually angelic Heart Beachy had somehow suddenly decided to find her voice, and it wasn't either angelic or timid.

Frankly, that young woman had a bit of a mouth on her.

When Levi was close enough for Mary to see the

deep lines around his eyes, and the worry and concern etched in those blue orbs, she felt her mouth go dry.

And right then and there she realized that Heart was not the only person who was wondering what was happening to her normally reserved emotions.

Because even though Mary's brain was telling her to focus on soothing this father-daughter relationship, all she currently was thinking about was just how gorgeous Levi Beachy was.

So tall. So strong. So . . . confident. He was everything her husband, Paul, had never been, and nothing that she'd ever thought she wanted. Well, that wasn't exactly true. Maybe, every once in a while, she'd imagined having such a man by her side in the middle of the night. When the sheets were cold and she was emotionally drained from helping someone depart this earth. On those nights, after she'd comforted the family and helped with the arrangements and finally returned home, she'd lie in her bed and imagine how nice it would be to have someone hold her tight. Someone who would whisper that he'd take all her troubles away.

No, that wasn't right.

She yearned for someone to reach out and help her carry her burdens. Not all the time. Just for a little while. Until she felt strong again.

Levi was that type of man. She knew it. But she'd never had any grand plans or dreams about having a relationship with him.

Yet, here she was.

Even though Heart was obviously worried, and Levi was obviously mad, Mary lifted her face to the sky.

God, what is going on with me? she silently asked. *Why Levi and why now?*

Only hearing Heart's whisper of a moan spurred Mary to get further involved than she already was. "Hello, Levi."

He stopped. Blinked. Clearly, he was taken off guard by the way she was greeting him, just as if they'd run into each other at the market. "Mary." He swallowed. "Any idea why Heart has come to you?"

She could practically feel Heart bristle next to her. Mary didn't fault her. "I reckon you should probably ask her that."

"Heart?" His voice had deepened.

The girl lifted her chin. "I don't know how I came to be here. I was walking and walking and somehow my feet found their way here."

He studied her for a long moment. Even in the dim light Mary could see Levi struggling with a response. "You had me worried, child."

"I know."

He pulled off his black knit cap and ran a hand through his dark blond hair before pulling it snug again over his ears. "I was so concerned about you going off in the dark, I left Clayton in the house." His lips twitched. "I fear he's probably talking with the rat right about now."

Heart's lips twitched. "Probably. Spike is good company."

Stepping closer to his daughter, he leaned down slightly so they were standing face-to-face. "Heart, you were right about the tablecloth. Your mother did like it and I did, too. I . . . I don't know why I got so upset about you putting it out."

"You miss Mamm."

"I do miss her, but it's not like I haven't come to terms with the fact that she's in Heaven. I know she's not coming back." He ran a hand over his short beard. "To be honest, I'd forgotten all about that cloth. I'm sorry for yelling at you."

"It's okay."

Looking even more puzzled, Levi added, "I'm not sure what has gotten into me of late. Everything that I've always taken as certain, now seems a bit different. I'm beginning to doubt myself. It's verra strange. It's like all my emotions have suddenly decided to overflow."

"I feel the same way," Heart said just as she launched herself into her father's arms.

Closing his eyes, he held her close. Rested his chin on the top of her bonnet. "You know I love you, Heart."

"I love you, too."

Watching them, Mary felt a lump in her throat. Levi and Heart had a special bond, and the awkward yet affectionate way Levi treated her was so sweet and tender.

When Heart pulled away from her father's chest, she smiled up at him, and then her eyes widened. "Oh! Clayton is here."

"What?" Levi dropped his arms and turned to face the man walking toward them.

Mary watched him approach. The young man's

steps looked almost as assured as Levi's had been. "It's like Grand Central Station around here," she joked.

"I'm going to see what he wants," Heart said as she hurried to meet him.

To Mary's surprise, Levi didn't follow. Instead, he remained by her side. Actually, he looked a bit amused.

Mary couldn't resist asking what he was thinking. "Why do you think Clayton is here, Levi?"

"I reckon either the barn is on fire or he was as worried about Heart as I was."

Or as worried about what Levi would do when he found his daughter as she'd been. "Let's hope and pray that it's the latter."

"*Jah*. A burned barn would be an inconvenience right now. What with me having an apprentice and all."

His irreverent comment spurred a burst of laughter. "Levi, are you joking?"

"It seems I am." He shook his head. "Like I said, my emotions have been running wild of late. I'm not sure what's going on. I can't even blame it on a full moon."

"Maybe it's because it's December and Christmas is approaching." That was her new excuse.

"Maybe. I couldn't say." His expression became impassive again as Clayton stepped forward, Heart by his side. "I'm surprised you found us, Clayton."

"It wasn't hard. There were two sets of footprints in the snow. I simply followed." Looking in Mary's direction, he nodded his head politely. "Hello. I'm Clayton Glick. I'm Levi's new apprentice."

"It's nice to meet you. I'm Mary Miller."

"Daed, Clayton said he'd walk me home. Do you mind?"

Levi stared hard at Clayton, but kept his voice soft for his daughter. "*Nee.* You two go on ahead. I need to speak to Mary for a moment."

"I'll keep her safe, sir."

A muscle in Levi's jaw jumped. "See that you do.". Just as they turned away, he called out, "Heart, you are holding Mary's cup. She'll be missing it."

Heart turned on her heel and hurried back. "Mary, I'm so sorry. Thank you for the hot chocolate and for the company." Reaching out, she hugged Mary tight. "And for the talk. You helped a lot."

"I'm glad I was here." Taking the cup, she looked at Clayton. "It was nice to meet you, Clayton."

"It was nice to meet you, too." He tipped his hat, but his eyes were already fastened on Heart.

When the girl walked to his side, his whole expression softened. When they turned and headed down the path, Mary noticed he stuffed his hands in his pockets. If she was a betting woman, she would say that he did that so he wouldn't inadvertently reach for the girl's hand.

"He's smitten, isn't he?" Levi asked.

Mary didn't want to make things worse for Clayton, but she couldn't deny what was in front of their eyes. "I'm afraid so. I don't think he's even noticing that it's snowing."

Levi grunted. "It sure doesn't look like it."

"Does that bother you?"

"Some." His mouth pursed, but he shrugged. "But

not as much as I would've thought. I can't really blame him, you see. My daughter is a beauty."

"She is. Just about every boy in Apple Creek has likely had a crush on her at one time or another."

"I don't know about that. She's only had one serious beau and he was worthless."

Mary couldn't help herself. She giggled. Like a young, giddy girl. Like the girl she never was. He blinked, obviously as surprised as she was by the sound. Mary supposed she should be embarrassed, but instead a feeling almost like triumph appeared. She had a crush on Levi Beachy and it made her happy. She was feeling things she hadn't since Paul died.

And, if she was honest, she'd never felt all that giddy around him. He'd been good to her. A lovely companion. She'd been happy with their life. But had she ever gotten a little flustered around him?

No. No, she had not.

A line formed between Levi's brows. Obviously, he was wondering what was going on with her. "Mary?"

"Levi, would you like to come in and see Virginia and her pups again? And maybe have a cup of hot chocolate before you head home?"

He hesitated. "I'll help you bring these two mugs inside, but then I'd better leave."

And . . . her giddy excitement tilted toward embarrassment. "Okay. Well—"

"If this boy is as smitten as we think, I'd best play chaperone."

He looked so serious. But maybe a little regretful, too?

"Of course." She smiled at him as he took Heart's mug out of her hand and accompanied her into the house.

They were two grown adults. She was a very capable woman. Neither mentioned that there was no reason on earth why he should help her walk an empty cup inside.

No reason except that he, too, wasn't eager to part ways.

She wasn't the only one who felt something.

A feeling of satisfaction appeared. She held it close, liking the way it felt. Yes. Something new was in the air.

Something delightful.

Chapter 16

It was dark, and the night closed around them, as only a winter night could. Because of the light snowfall there wasn't even a brave star or the sliver of moonlight lighting their way.

Clayton was grateful for the flashlight he'd grabbed from a cubby near the stationary tub. It emitted a weak, wan light, but it was enough.

"It's a good thing we aren't wise men, ain't so?" he joked. "We'd have quite a time searching for baby Jesus."

"*Jah.* I, um, read somewhere that the Wise Men had been searching for years for the Messiah and that their celebration had as much to do with their own exhaustion as it did with the birth of Jesus. Do you think that's true?"

"I'm not sure, though I kind of hope so. I like the idea of not being the only person searching for something for a very long time."

"What have you been searching for?"

You. Your father. A home. "Oh, I don't know." Why he had decided to share that snippet while walking in the cold and dark, he didn't know. "Are you doing okay?"

"Well enough."

"*Gut.* What do you think? Are we about halfway back to your house?"

"*Jah.* But it's *our* house now, right?"

It was as if she'd read his mind. "I don't think we're quite there yet," he said lightly.

"What have you been searching for, Clayton?"

Maybe it was the dark or the fact that they were alone, or that he'd been so worried about her that some of his defenses had dissolved. "A home," he whispered.

"I'm glad you found one with me."

He swallowed. Surely, she'd misspoken. Had meant at their farm. In a general sense. Yes. Heart hadn't meant to sound so personal.

He was sure she'd had no idea that her words had hit him the way they had, either. But whether she had or not, her sweet statement filled his soul . . . and spurred him to speak again.

"When I was about nine, I started to realize it wasn't very likely that a couple was ever going to want to adopt me. So, um, I started to change my wishes. Instead of hoping and praying for parents of my own, I began wishing for a place of my own. Somewhere that was just mine. Private." Thinking of the large room with the six beds in it, he murmured, "Sometimes I just wanted to be alone, with only my thoughts for company."

"Isn't that something? I've been blessed with so much, but I was always yearning not to be alone." She chuckled. "I guess we were meant to find each other."

Her words were perfect. And as far as he was concerned, true. But how did he respond? They hadn't known each other for very long at all. Certainly not long enough for her father to accept him as a suitor. Plus, he was still trying to find his footing and learn how to be a good smith. He had practically nothing of worth to offer her.

So, like a scared boy, he kept his mouth shut, searching his mind for something to say the way the thin beam of light was searching for their footpath.

A new, awkward tension filled the air. Heart curved her arms around herself. Maybe because she was cold. Maybe because she felt his distance.

And then she tripped.

"Oh!" A little too slowly, she released her hands to break her fall. Heart would've fallen if he hadn't been right there to catch her.

He grasped her close. "It's okay. I've got ya."

When she trembled in his arms, he rubbed his hand along her back. Supposedly to warm her up. Or comfort her. Or because he didn't have the right words in his head, but his arms seemed to know that she needed his support. As each second passed, she seemed to lean closer to him, almost resting her entire body against his. She felt precious.

"Are you okay?" he finally asked. Once he'd found his voice again.

"Yes. I should've been watching where I was walking," she murmured into his neck.

"It's dark and the ground is hard to see. It's slick in spots, too." He rolled his eyes. Leave it to him to concentrate on the weather conditions.

Heart lifted her chin. "Thank you for catching me."

That was his signal to release her. With reluctance he dropped his hands. Forced himself to step back. The cold air enveloped him again. "Of course."

"We should continue. If we tarry too much longer, my father will catch up with us."

"Yes." The very last thing he needed was for Levi to see his precious daughter wrapped in Clayton's arms.

They'd taken just a couple of steps when he noticed her trembling again. She was cold.

He took off his coat and placed it around her shoulders.

Even in the dim light he noticed that she held it to her. "*Danke*, but you need this."

"I don't." This small thing made him happy. He was helping her. Keeping her warm. Protecting her from the elements. When she shifted, obviously ready to protest again, he cut her off. "Don't say it."

"Say what?"

"That I need it back. I don't."

"It's freezing out here. Snowing. You're in shirt-sleeves. You don't even have any gloves on."

"I have a wool cap on my head. I'm fine." When she appeared ready to argue, he added, "Keep walking. Remember, we don't have much farther."

She walked on. "This is a surprise."

"What is?"

"I didn't think you were the bossy sort."

"Why? Because I don't argue with your father?"

She chuckled under her breath. "No. Sorry, but no one argues with him."

"No one except for his daughter. Ain't so?"

She chuckled. "I don't usually. I . . . I just was tired of holding my tongue." She sighed. "I can't believe I ran off like a spoiled girl who didn't get her way."

He moved a pine branch out of her way, then gave in to temptation and reached for her elbow. Despite all the layers he could feel her bicep contract, then relax as she became accustomed to the touch.

Another dash of satisfaction coursed through him. She was allowing his touch again.

Heart had sped up her pace, which was no problem for him, since he was in boots and had been walking slowly to stay by her side. But she was in delicate-looking black boots. She was going to slip on a patch of ice or a fallen pinecone or something if she wasn't careful.

"Careful now," he whispered.

"Yes."

He ached to say something else. Oh, nothing about

her safety or the cold. But something interesting. Something that, perhaps, would make her take another look at him. Think that maybe he was something more than her father's apprentice. Something besides a stranger to whom she'd been kind enough to offer a warm bed and a comfortable room.

Unfortunately, he had nothing of interest in his head. Maybe it was simply the cold, but it seemed he was currently devoid of all thought.

They continued to walk, carefully moving through the snow, patches of ice, and occasional fallen branches. Now they were about two-thirds of the way back to the Beachys' homestead, though it was hard to judge. The way felt longer, since he was no longer worried about her being out on her own. It was infinitely more pleasant, however—and who could blame him for thinking that? He still had hold of her arm. It now seemed as if she was almost relying on his assistance. It pleased him.

"Hey, Clayton?" Heart asked after another five or seven minutes passed.

"Jah?"

"Do you think I'm terrible?"

Since all his thoughts had pretty much been focused on just how perfect he thought she was, the question caught him off guard. "Of course not," he blurted. "Why would you ask such a thing?"

"Because I ran off like I did, making both you and Daed come find me. It was irresponsible."

He glanced down at her, moving the flashlight's beam a bit. Hoping to get a hint of what was behind the question from her expression, but Heart was looking straight ahead.

It seemed he was on his own.

"First of all, I had nothing better to do. So chasing after you gave me a much-needed purpose."

"Don't joke." She tried to pull her arm from his grasp. "I'm being serious."

Although he didn't want to hurt her, he couldn't help but tighten his hold. "I'm sorry if you don't think I'm taking you seriously. I am." When she yanked her arm again, he made himself drop his hand, giving her the freedom she sought. "Heart, you were right about the tablecloth. I didn't know my parents, but if I did, I would've wanted something to remember them by. Putting a tablecloth on a table at Christmas isn't too much to ask."

"Even though it isn't all that Plain?"

He couldn't resist rolling his eyes. "Oh, please. Your father designs large metal structures that are anything but Plain. Ninety-nine percent of his customers are *English*. If he was such a stickler for things like that, he would be . . . Oh, I don't know. Only shoeing horses."

"I never thought about it that way."

"I don't know if your father's job has a lot to do with keeping a proper Amish house, but I have to think that he couldn't have thought too differently when your mother was alive. Did he?"

"Nee."

"Do you remember him getting upset with your *mamm* when she put out her Christmas tablecloth?"

"He never did. He would just smile at her. My father

is cranky with just about everyone, but he never was with her. He loved her a lot."

"He loves you, too."

Heart nodded, but it was obvious she was still thinking about her memories. "Mamm used to be so happy in December. She used to hug him and say that Christmas was her favorite time of the year." She inhaled. "Oh!"

"There you go," he whispered. "I don't think he was upset with you so much as hurting."

"You're right. Because that tablecloth brings back memories he's tried to push aside."

"It brings back good memories, Heart. That's why he fought you a bit, I think. The memories are sweet for him."

"And painful."

"Maybe so."

She glanced up at him. "What do you think I should do?"

"What did he say when he found you?"

"That I can put the tablecloth on. That he was wrong."

"I think you should put it on, then."

"It's that easy?"

"*Nee*. I don't think it will be easy at all . . . but maybe it doesn't have to be. Maybe all that matters is that you are making the choice to move on and be happy."

"Clayton."

"Disagree if you like. I won't fault you for that. But all I'm saying is that good things don't necessarily feel good at first, but they're worth it. If you put out some of your mother's things, it might feel a little uncomfortable this year, but perhaps next year, when you bring them up from the basement, there will be some good memories, too."

"Clayton, you're right." Her voice was bright.

Then, wonder of wonders, she curved her gloved hand around his bicep.

And his muscle contracted at her touch, just as hers had.

"I'm so glad we talked," she added.

"Me too." Seeing her house up ahead, and not hearing her father's steps behind him, he covered her hand with his own.

When she didn't pull her hand away, he smiled to himself. And thanked the good Lord for giving him the words to help Heart. And, perhaps, himself as well.

Chapter 17

The first thing the next morning, after Heart got dressed and said her prayers, she threw on a wool shawl and hurried outside to gather eggs from the henhouse. Of late, Clayton had taken over the chore, but she was of a mind to do something special for breakfast.

Besides, though the hens weren't her favorite creatures in the world, she did enjoy their cantankerous squawking and fussing from time to time.

Then, as she'd done for the last three years at least once a month, she began making a platter of eggs-in-a-hole. When she'd been small, she'd been as enchanted about the stack of neatly toasted circles as she had been about the slices of toast that each held one perfectly fried egg in its center. Mamm had even let her stand on a chair to watch them cook, chuckling when Heart used to clap when they were done.

It wasn't until Heart began making the dish on her own that she'd realized toasting the bread and cooking the egg perfectly took a bit of practice.

Heart still grimaced every time she thought about the first attempts she'd made for her father. The bread had been either burned or greasy. Likewise, the eggs had either turned out to be too runny or so overdone that they had more in common with rubber hockey pucks than eggs. To his credit, he'd eaten those early attempts without complaint. But even she had a difficult time stomaching her failures.

Nowadays she could practically make eggs-in-a-hole in her sleep. She was glad of that this morning because she was exhausted. She'd tossed and turned all night—running over her actions and words the evening before.

And the way Clayton had treated her.

Heart couldn't help it, she'd been grateful for his kindness. A little bit confused, too. Billy Weaver had never treated her with such care.

Now she realized that Billy had likely never thought too much about her. Not really. Only that she was Levi Beachy's daughter and that there were rumors Levi was a wealthy man. He'd either fawned over her father or been afraid of him. Yet, whenever he was alone with her, he'd seemed to hardly know what to say.

She realized now that had been for the best. Billy

hadn't been the man for her. God really knew what He was doing when He didn't answer prayers.

When the back door opened, she listened for the telltale thud of her father's boots.

Instead, she heard the sounds of someone taking off boots and gloves.

"Gut matin," Clayton said as he strode into the kitchen. On his feet were thick socks, one of which had a small hole near the big toe.

"Good morning." She smiled at him as she carefully flipped the pieces of toast on the cast-iron skillet. "I thought you were still abed."

He grinned. "I've been up for two hours."

"Doing what? I didn't see you when I gathered eggs."

"I started the forge for the day and mucked out a few of the horse stalls."

"What is my *daed* doing?"

"I believe he's in his office, doing some paperwork or some such."

"Ah." After she peeked at the toast, she decided it was ready, then pulled out three plates. "It's time to eat."

For the first time he glanced at the two skillets on the gas range. "What is that?"

"Eggs-in-a-hole." She smiled at him. "I guess you've never had them before?"

"I have not." He was staring at the creations as if she'd done something amazing. "Those are cute."

Cute? The things he said. She laughed. "I've never

heard them described as such. I hope you think they're good."

"I'm starting to realize that I'll like anything you make, Heart."

There went that flutter inside again. "Sit down when you are ready. You need to eat while it's warm."

"What about your father? Should I go fetch him?"

She looked at the clock. "Let's wait a moment. Daed rarely forgets his mealtimes."

After carrying the platter to the table, she added the sausages and two cups of coffee. Then she sat down with a sigh. It was a new day. Time for a fresh start.

She sure needed it.

Last night when they'd gotten home, she'd been exhausted. The moment she'd walked in the door, she'd spread the tablecloth on the table, smoothed it out, and then started crying.

Clayton, of course, had been worried, but her father had taken her tears even more to heart.

Which had made her feel even worse.

She'd ended up excusing herself early, electing to take a hot bath, put on her favorite flannel nightgown, and then sit in bed with a library book. Her plan had been to focus on the storyline instead of her own problems.

She'd only made it through two pages before she'd fallen into a fitful slumber. But the Lord was good. Instead of being groggy, she'd been able to get up early and prepare breakfast.

"Ah, eggs-in-a-hole," her father said as he burst into

the room, his boots once again tracking snow across the floor. "This makes me happy. Thank you, daughter."

"You're welcome."

A minute later, after Clayton returned from washing up, he joined them. First the three silently gave thanks; then they dug in.

As was their habit, neither she nor her father said much. Clayton seemed to have no problem with their quiet breakfast, either.

She ate one portion of the egg dish, but skipped the sausage, preferring to sip her coffee as she watched the men.

Her father ate three eggs. Clayton ate two, then had another after she promised that she didn't want any more.

And then, less than fifteen minutes after she'd taken the food off the griddle, they were done.

Her father scooted his chair back. "Two of my art clients will be here today, Heart."

"What time?"

"One in about an hour, the other around two. I already told Clayton to watch for them, but if you see them first, take them to the barn."

"I will."

"We're also expecting Jed with two of his plow horses."

"Would you like me to watch for him?" Clayton asked.

"Jed knows where to go," Heart supplied. "He's been a customer of Daed's for a long time."

Her father nodded. "He has. You'll likely hear the horse trailer, Clayton. Unless we're working at the forge."

"Yes, sir."

Walking to the back door, her father paused again. "Breakfast was good, Heart."

"*Danke*, Daed."

He paused again. "So . . . dinner at eleven?"

"*Jah*, Father. Just like always."

He searched her face. Heart knew he was looking for signs that everything between them was good again. When she smiled at him, he seemed to relax. "Okay, then. *Gut.* Clayton, you coming?"

"Yes, sir. I'll be right there. I'm going to help Heart clear the table first."

Her father poked his head back into the kitchen. "Why?"

"Because she has enough to do, ain't so?"

Her father looked confused, then took a longer look at the two skillets on the range and the three plates and cups on the table. "Hmm. I reckon so." The back door closed seconds later.

When they were alone, Clayton reached for a pan. "Would you like me to wash the skillets . . . or clean the floor? What will help you the most?"

She appreciated his gesture, but it wasn't necessary. "Neither."

"Why?"

"Clayton, this is my job. Not yours."

"I know, but it's important to me to help you."

"But you are here to apprentice with my *daed*."

"Your father is fine. His shop is ready. He can wait another ten minutes while I help you."

"I don't understand why you'd want to do that, though."

"Because I can," he murmured. "That's why. I can and so I will. Now tell me what to do."

She was just about to point to the skillets when she heard a rustling from Spike's cage. "You may collect Spike and bring him over here. I have a few pieces of fruit for him."

"You'd rather I feed your rat instead of wash pans?"

"Yes."

When he hesitated, she playfully batted her eyes at him. "You offered to help me. This is what I'd like you to do."

"All right, then."

Watching him walk to Spike's cage, open it, then speak quietly to the rat before gently enfolding it in one hand, Heart felt her stomach do a little somersault.

She told herself it was happiness because she was so pleased to have a pet at last.

She didn't think even Spike would believe that.

Chapter 18

It was three o'clock and Clayton's head was spinning. He'd now been working at the Beachy farm for over a week. Every day had gotten a little bit easier. Clayton had begun to gain confidence and Levi had begun to give him more and more responsibility.

They were also forming a relationship.

Clayton wouldn't call it anything close to father and son, but it did feel—at least to him—much more than just apprentice and boss. Their exchanges had become comfortable.

This Thursday was the first time that Levi had allowed him to stay by his side while he talked to his art clients and met with the farmers and ranchers who needed new shoes for their horses.

Through it all, Levi was the same man that he always was. He listened intently, was blunt with his words and answers, and gentle with both his artwork and the horses.

He introduced everyone to Clayton, telling each customer that Clayton was his apprentice and could be trusted . . . but also that he didn't know too much yet.

If Clayton had had any grand ideas about his worth, they would have surely vanished by the time Levi had introduced him the third time. However, instead of feeling worse about himself, he'd ended up feeling almost better. It was good to know that Levi didn't have too many expectations that he couldn't meet or exceed. He was also quickly learning that Heart had been right. Her father's bark really was worse than his bite. As long as Clayton worked hard and tried his best, Levi had no problems with him.

When Levi insisted on being the one to transport the metal sculpture to his last client of the day, Clayton decided to make himself useful. He put a bridle on Becket, walked him out of his stall, and then, after loosely tying his lead around a pole, he got out a currycomb and brush and began to methodically groom the gelding.

Becket shied away from him at first, but then began to lean toward him as his trust in Clayton grew. By the time he had lifted one of the horse's hooves and cleaned it, he knew Becket and he were going to be fast friends.

"This is *gut, jah?*" he murmured as he moved on to the next hoof. "You're a beauty. Someone needed to give you a touch of TLC, I think."

Becket was nodding his head when Levi strode back in.

His boss looked taken aback by the sight of Clayton grooming his horse, but his expression softened as he stepped closer.

"It seems that this is Becket's lucky day."

Clayton shrugged. "I don't know if he is going to consider a good brushing as such, but it was needed, I think."

Levi folded his arms across his chest as he watched Clayton. "Where did you learn to groom horses? At the children's home?"

"*Jah.* There, and at some of the nearby farms where I worked after I left."

"You're good with animals. I'm surprised you don't want to work at a stable or at a large farm."

"I fear I let my emotions get the best of me. I never enjoyed taking animals to market or slaughtering them."

Levi pursed his lips. "I know what you mean. It's easier to work with objects that one doesn't grow attached to, ain't so?"

"It was for me." He walked Becket back into his stall. The horse also looked pleased that Clayton had taken the time to clean the straw and give him fresh water. He gently butted Clayton's side with his head and swished his tail.

Clayton laughed. "You're welcome, horse."

Levi grinned, obviously enjoying Becket's antics. "Clayton, I think it's time you began a project of your own. Don't you?"

That caught him off guard. "More horseshoes?"

"Horseshoes have their purpose, but I was thinking of something more along the lines of a piece of art."

"What?"

"You told me that art was your ultimate goal, yes?"

"Yes, but—"

"No buts. I think you are ready. Pull out one of the drawings you showed me the other day. We've time today to come up with a plan."

"Which design should I work on?" Thinking about the drawings he'd shown Levi, Clayton was torn between what he wanted to do and what he was afraid to attempt in front of Levi. That was the problem with having a mentor one admired, he decided. He didn't want to embarrass himself in front of him.

"It's not up to me. It's up to you, Clayton. You're the artist of your designs."

There it was again: temptation to push himself, accompanied by the stark fear of embarrassment. He swallowed. "Some of my designs are going to be harder to execute than others. I don't know if I am capable of making what I want." He steeled himself. "To be honest, I don't know if I'll ever have the skills needed to be a good smith or a good welder. I know you're one of the most talented craftsmen around, so it ain't right to compare myself to you. Sometimes I feel like I'm fooling myself."

"Why?"

"Maybe I'll never be good at any of this."

Glad that he'd finally shared his worries, he held his breath and waited to hear what Levi had to say. He knew he needed to be prepared for Levi to give him some hard truths—to remind him that he wasn't even making a perfect horseshoe yet. That he had no business taking on something more difficult.

Instead, his voice was as mild as ever. "Where are your designs, Clayton? Are they in the house?"

"*Nee.* They're in the loft." When Levi raised an eyebrow, Clayton explained himself. "I was sweeping up there and noticed the drawer in the bedside table. I figured you wouldn't mind if I used it."

"Go get your tablet and we'll look at them together."

Clayton felt like a kid as he hurried out of the room, past the horse stalls, and climbed up the ladder. He barely looked at the clean, organized space before retracing his steps, this time with his drawing pad in his hands.

Levi's eyes lit up when Clayton returned. He had on glasses and was studying a drawing of his own. "Pick out three ideas that you're keen about. Not the ones that look the simplest, the three that you think will make you happiest to do."

"All right." Feeling Levi's eyes on him, he flipped pages.

"Take a moment, son," Levi cautioned. Lowering his voice, he added, "I know what you are doing. You're thinking of me and what you think I'd like to see." He shook his head. "Take me out of it. Say a prayer, think of your hands and your heart, and choose."

He had almost thirty designs sketched out. Clayton realized with some surprise that he'd felt passionate about each of them at one time or another. "You make choosing favorites sound so easy."

"It is. You've got good hands and a long life ahead of you. I'm not saying you can only make three of them. I'm advising you to pick three to work on first. That's it."

"All right." Clayton flipped through his drawings with more ease, but there was still a bit of a tremor in his hands. He was nervous. He was nervous to put his dreams on display for Levi. They meant so much to him.

"Gut." Levi glanced out the open door of his work-room. "I'm going to check on Heart and get us something to drink. Then I'll be back."

Once Levi left the room, Clayton did what he'd suggested. He closed his eyes and asked the Lord for His help. Asked Him to think of his strengths and his weaknesses . . . and where his heart lay.

And, suddenly, his choices felt easier.

When Levi returned, he was grinning. "I got us some sodas."

Clayton gaped at the pair of light green cans in his hands. "Mountain Dew?"

"I know. But this is a big event, I think. I thought we might need to have a little boost in honor of it. Or . . . you can continue to drink water. It's your choice."

He held out his hand. "This decision ain't hard. Thank you for the soda."

Levi's eyes brightened. "You're welcome."

"What did Heart say? I can't believe she has cans of soda hidden away in the kitchen."

"I think she might have forgotten about them. And, just so you know, Heart didn't say anything about the drinks because I didn't tell her. She was sitting on the couch with that foolish rat and a book."

"Heart likes Spike a lot."

"Indeed." His focus shifted to the open notepad. "Did you pick three?"

"I did." After taking a fortifying sip of the soda, Clayton showed Levi his choices. One was a metal bar with a diamond cut out of the middle. He'd added three hooks, making it into a key holder. "Here's the first."

"All right. What's next?"

He flipped the pages. "This one," he said. "It's kind of like a large die, but with cutouts on each face instead of dots."

"And your third?"

Clayton had hoped that Levi would've given him some kind of feedback about the die, but bit back his disappointment. He was supposed to be thinking about himself, not Levi's approval. He flipped through more pages until he came to his last choice. Staring at the design, which was a large, open heart balanced on its side, he felt his stomach do a little somersault of nerves. "This."

"Ah."

Clayton looked up at Levi. "What do you think?"

"I think you've got three very different choices."

"Which do you think I should do? You're the artist—I'd like your opinion."

Levi stuffed his hands in his pockets. "It's up to you, but I think there's one that speaks to you the most."

"Which one?" He was pretty sure it wasn't the key ring, so it was either the die or the heart.

"Come now, boy. You know the truth. I saw it in your eyes when you turned the page. Stop thinking so much and say it."

"The heart."

Approval gleamed in Levi's eyes. "Good for you. Let's get to work."

Clayton had once thought the best day of his life was when Rachel had let him sneak a kiss behind the schoolhouse when they were thirteen. He'd changed his mind when he'd gotten his first paycheck and Garrett had taken him to the bank to help him set up his own account.

That moment had paled when he'd received the letter stating that Levi Beachy had consented to mentor him.

But none of those instances compared to the feeling of satisfaction he was experiencing at that moment. At long last, in spite of many obstacles, he was getting the opportunity to make his dreams a reality.

His insides felt like a pinball machine. Satisfaction, hope, happiness, nervousness—they all zipped inside him.

No matter what happened in the future, even if he failed to become an artist, Clayton knew he'd never forget this moment. Never in a million years.

Chapter 19

The boy had talent. There was no doubt about it. Watching Clayton carefully use the torch in his hand to cut the metal, Levi noticed that he had a steady, sure hand. He also had a new intensity about him that had nothing to do with Levi's approval, or even the fact that he'd already improved a lot since his first day.

When the three-foot piece had been neatly sliced, Levi showed him how to make the edges more refined. "Like this," he said as he demonstrated. "See the difference?"

"*Jah.*"

When Clayton gripped the torch again and mimicked Levi's movement, the metal complied.

"Very good. It's better."

Holding the metal in between his gloved hands, Clayton grinned as he examined every inch. "It is, isn't it?"

It was good to hear pride in the boy's voice. "See how this part isn't as sharp? That ain't easy to do."

"I couldn't have done it without your help."

"That's why you're an apprentice, *jah?* I'm supposed to be teaching you a thing or two."

Clayton grinned. "I'd say you've taught me more than just a couple of things so far."

Levi clapped him on the back. "I was pleased to do it. Now I think it's time to call it a day. Turn off the torch and let's clean up."

Clayton looked like a little boy being told that it was time to go home from the fair. "Are you sure we have to stop right now? Maybe—"

"I'm sure. Look at the time."

Clayton eyed the clock. "It's half past four."

"*Jah.* Which means Heart will have supper on the table in thirty minutes. We canna disrespect her by being late."

To Levi's amusement, Clayton appeared to be weighing his response, but he did turn off the torch. "It's easy for time to get the best of me."

"It is. There's been many a day when I wasn't ready to stop. But I have to admit that it's never a bad thing to call it quits before one gets too tired. Fixing welding mistakes isn't easy."

"No, I don't guess it is."

"I'll bank the fire in the forge, you put away the

tools and clean the rest. You did good today. Not just with your design, either. You were good with customers and the horses."

"Thank you. I want to do a good job."

"That isn't a worry," he said as he focused on tamping the fire. "See you inside. Don't be late."

"I won't."

Levi felt a burst of satisfaction as he walked out of the barn. The Lord had been right when He'd guided him to answer the note from the home about the boy's apprenticeship. He had talent and was a good worker.

He'd also noticed that Clayton wasn't oblivious to Heart. Not by a long shot. Heart also seemed to return the feelings.

It was a bit of a shock, but he didn't hate the idea that the two of them seemed to be smitten with each other. His daughter likely thought he was unaware of the struggles she'd experienced since her mother's passing, but they hadn't slipped his notice. He'd spent many of his middle-of-the-night wanderings thinking about her.

His problem had never been that he didn't realize she'd been unhappy; it was that he'd had no idea how to make things better for her. Katie had been her daughter's confidante and advisor. Levi had taught Heart how to do small tasks in his workshop, but his main job had been to give her hugs and "fix" all her injuries.

Whenever she'd had a splinter or a cut, she'd run to him. No matter what he'd been doing—even if it had been talking to a fancy client—he'd attended to her. Heart was his girl, and it was his job to heal her hurts.

The physical ones, at least.

The emotional ones? They'd often remained a mystery.

Right now, he didn't necessarily believe that Clayton was going to solve all her problems, but at least this man was nearby and was decent.

No. To be fair, the pup was more than that. Clayton Glick was a good man. A good man who'd had more than his fair share of heartaches and challenges, but didn't dwell on them. Instead, he worked every day to become something better. Heart could do far worse.

When he opened the back door, he smiled to himself as he removed his boots and even went so far as to wash his hands in the stationary tub by the door. Just as he was pulling off a paper towel to dry his hands, he heard his daughter cry out.

"Heart?" he called as he strode into the kitchen. "What happened? Did you cut yourself?"

"Nee."

He looked around. It took a second for him to realize that she wasn't in the kitchen as usual. "Where are ya?"

"Living room."

"What happened?" Seeing her on the floor, he hurried to her side. "What happened?" he asked as he grasped her shoulders. "Did you fall? Are you ill?"

"Daed, your hands are strong, *jah?*"

"Sorry." Afraid that he'd hurt her, he drew his hands back. "Where do you hurt?" Maybe she was having an appendicitis attack? Or some mysterious female ailment? "Darling, do you need me to get Mary?"

"Mary? *Nee.*"

"You don't think she'd understand?" He really was trying to figure out what was ailing his daughter.

"She'd understand, but I don't think she'd appreciate what I'm going through."

Ah. It was that time of the month. He might be a man, but he'd been married, and hadn't been completely oblivious to a teenage Heart lying on the couch with a heating pad a time or two.

Feeling slightly better about the situation, he tried to stop his blushes. "I'm sure Mary would. I have a feeling it's a common enough occurrence."

Heart lifted her head. "Do you truly think so?"

He was in over his head, but he could do this. "*Jah*, sure. I'm no expert, of course." Reaching for her again, he murmured, "Let's get you to a chair. Or maybe you want to lie down?" He tried to think back to the things Katie had done for her. "I know, a hot bath?"

Heart froze before twisting to face him. "Daed, I canna lie down. Spike is missing."

"Wait. That's what you're talking about? The rat?"

"Well, *jah*. What did you think was wrong?"

He sat back on his heels. "I thought it was some type of female ailment." He waved a hand. "You know . . ."

Heart's blue eyes widened. "Oh, Daed. No."

He was sure he hadn't blushed so much since the first time he'd tried to kiss Katie and ended up knocking his teeth into hers. "It was an honest mistake."

Her lips twitched. "Not really."

"Come on." He was embarrassed now, but at least Heart was amused instead of turning beet red.

She covered her mouth. "Sorry, but I don't recall

Mamm or Mary or me ever being reduced to crawling
on the floor because of a monthly bout of cramps."

"Come to think of it, I don't, either." He chuckled.
He'd been a fool.

"Oh, Daed."

And then, to his surprise, Heart burst out in laughter. He couldn't help but join in. Laughing felt so good,
was so freeing, tears formed in the corners of his eyes.
Figuring there was no reason to fight it, he sat on the
floor and continued laughing.

"Hello?" Clayton called out.

"We're in here, Clayton," he replied.

Walking in, Clayton looked at the couch, then fastened his gaze on the two of them sitting on the floor.
Levi knew they were a sight. He still had tears in his
eyes and Heart's face was flushed.

"Hiya, Clayton," Heart said.

One second passed. Then two. Finally Clayton spoke.
"Ah, is everything all right?"

"Not really," Heart replied. "Spike escaped."

He walked toward them slowly, whether because he
was worried about stepping on the rat or because he
was worried about their state of minds was anyone's
guess. "So, you both are looking for him under the coffee table?"

"I was," Heart said. "I mean, I've been looking everywhere."

When Clayton glanced his way, Levi chuckled. "It's
a long story, but I thought Heart was injured. It turns
out she's fine."

"Okay, then." To Levi's amusement, the boy knelt

down beside them. "Which direction should I look? Heart, did you see him around here?"

"Um, maybe?"

As answers went, it was a bad one. However, Levi's daughter's nonanswer seemed to satisfy Clayton just fine. He placed both palms on the floor.

"Which way do you want me to look?" Clayton asked.

"You've been working all day. I know you usually like to go straight to the shower. Are you sure you don't mind?"

"Verra sure."

Heart's expression melted. "That's so nice of you."

Satisfied that the two of them had the search and rescue under control, Levi got to his feet. "Since Clayton's going to take over, I'll go take my shower. Good luck finding Spike."

Heart's voice rose. "You're just going to leave, Daed?"

"For sure and for certain. I'm a sweaty mess." He wasn't, really, but whatever.

"But what if—"

"If I see Spike in the shower, I'll let you know," he called out as he left the room.

When Levi closed his bedroom door, he found himself chuckling again. He didn't know when he'd ever laughed so much. Had he ever?

He couldn't even remember losing control like that when he was a boy.

But instead of feeling ashamed about losing his dignity, he was brought up short by the realization. Why hadn't he ever let go of his control enough to feel such joy? He didn't know.

Yet, here he was, in his late forties, and he was discovering things to be happy about all the time. It was a real shame that he'd waited so long.

Laughter felt good. It felt cleansing. Hopeful, even. The Lord sure worked in amazing ways. Even, it seemed, in the form of a rat.

"Daed, are you already in the shower?" Heart called from the other side of his bedroom door.

"Not yet." Suddenly worrying that they'd found Spike's body instead of a living, wandering rodent, he turned to the door. "Everything okay?"

"*Jah*. We found him!" Heart called out. "He's just fine, too. I don't think he's any the worse for wear after his adventure. Don't worry, Daed!"

"Good to hear it!" As if he'd been worrying about the rat's well-being. Well, not too much, anyway.

Chuckling again, Levi strode into his well-appointed bathroom. It looked like Heart and Clayton had everything in hand. No further input from him was necessary.

Chapter 20

It had been several long days for Mary, too. Just a few days after Heart, Levi, and Clayton had come over in the middle of a snowstorm, she'd been asked to help an *English* family who lived just outside of Wooster. Their seven-year-old son, Gary, had broken his leg riding a skateboard, and his mother had asked Mary to come over for a few hours every day to help Gary get around the house while she went to work.

Gary was a sweet boy and fun to be with, but he was also every bit of seven. Once his pain had lessened and the novelty of having a cast had worn off, he was quickly bored. Mary had had her hands full attempting to entertain him. Ironically, even though his parents had bought him an electronic tablet filled with all sorts of games, the child had enjoyed playing cards with her the most. She'd ended up making bowls of popcorn, sipping hot chocolate, and playing game after game of Uno with him.

Barely twenty-four hours after she'd concluded that job, Flora Hochstetler had knocked on Mary's door. The doctor had said that her husband Jerry's time was near. Jerry had been battling a number of ailments for years, and they'd finally gotten the best of him. The family now needed Mary's services in order to get through his last days.

Mary loved her job. She liked Flora and Jerry very much and was glad that she could help make this difficult time easier to bear.

But she still had a litter of puppies to care for and was trying to get her house together after working with Gary for five hours a day. In addition, Levi had stopped by . . . yet again.

This time he'd only stayed a half hour. He said he'd needed a break and couldn't think of a better way to relax than taking a short walk and spending a few minutes with her. Mary knew part of the draw was also the coffee and cookies she always had on hand—as well as Virginia's affectionate, adorable puppies. But sometimes, when he stared at her intently, she forgot about that.

By the time he'd left, she was a bundle of nerves. All she'd wanted to do was sit at home, help Virginia, and try to figure out what was going on between her and the big man.

Obviously, God had other plans, because Flora practically arrived on Levi's heels.

"I'll be happy to help you and Jerry," she said after serving Flora a slice of cinnamon swirl bread and a cup of fresh coffee. "I'm going to need to stop by here, one or two times a day, though. Virginia and her puppies can't stay on their own."

Suddenly spying the puppies, who were now far more eager to explore and play than they'd been two weeks ago, Flora smiled. "They are adorable, aren't they?" She walked over to the area that Mary had only recently blocked off with a baby gate, and the older woman's face eased into a beautiful smile. "I've been so consumed with Jerry's ills, I'd almost forgotten that the Lord brings miracles into our midst all the time."

When one of the pups hurried over to her, obviously anxious to get some attention, Flora knelt down and picked him up. "Aren't you a dear?"

The puppy yipped and tried to chew her finger.

"Careful," Mary warned. "Their teeth are tiny but sharp."

"I'll be careful, but these old hands are tougher than they look." After a spell she glanced at Mary. "I'm sure you don't want to leave them."

"I want to be there for you and Jerry. I'm going to ask Heart Beachy if she'll stop by to help out."

Flora's lined face eased into a bright smile. "Heart would do a wonderful-*gut* job with the pups. Do you think Levi will be able to get along without her?"

"*Jah.* Especially since he has an apprentice now."

"I heard about that. He's a young, strapping lad, *jah?*"

Mary laughed. "That describes him perfectly."

"All the girls in the area have been eyeing him at church. He better get ready."

"I agree." Although she had a feeling that Clayton wouldn't notice any girl other than Heart. "Flora, expect me tomorrow morning. I'll talk to Heart this afternoon and get myself together this evening."

"*Danke*, Mary." After cuddling the pup for a few more minutes, Flora took her leave.

Soon after that, Mary put on her cloak, a black bonnet over her *kapp*, her new red-and-green gloves, and headed over to the Beachy farm. It was going to be her first visit since she was there for Katie's last days on earth. She wasn't sure how it would feel to be there again. Actually, how she would feel around Levi. Things between them had changed. She'd gone from believing him to be the type of man to kill a pet rat, to hoping they'd have an opportunity to spend more time together.

Since she'd never been one to make rash judgments, Mary wondered what had happened. Had her feelings about him flipped quickly? Or had their relationship—and the way she thought about him—changed gradually without her taking note of it?

The man himself was outside shoveling when she walked up the driveway. At first, Levi didn't seem to be aware of her approach. He'd taken off his wool coat. She noticed the tails of his gray shirt were untucked and the navy sweater he was wearing on top of it was worn and stretched. His head was down and he was methodically shoveling snow, tossing it over his shoulder, and then scooping again. The amount he was clearing was not small. She wouldn't have been able to lift a third as much easily.

Only after ten or fifteen tosses did Levi stop for a breather. And then he spied her. "Mary?" He tossed the snow shovel into the middle of the snowbank he'd just made and headed her way.

She raised a hand. "Hiya, Levi."

The closer he got, the more his expression seemed to be etched with concern. "Is everything all right? Do you need something?"

"*Danke*, but I actually came to beg a favor from Heart. Is she inside the house?"

He didn't move. "She is. What do you need?"

"Help with Virginia and the pups." Figuring he would learn the news soon, anyway, she added, "Jerry Hochstetler is doing poorly. The doctors told Flora that he'll be heading to Heaven soon."

"Now, that's too bad." Eyes full of compassion, he murmured, "He's put up a good fight, hasn't he?"

She nodded. "He has. Flora stopped by to ask if I can attend to him so he won't have to leave the house. I said I would, starting tomorrow morning. But I'm going to need help. I can't take Virginia with me or the pups. I was going to ask my neighbor to watch them, but I started thinking that Heart might be a better choice. She is so good with Virginia."

"I agree." He led the way into the house. To her amusement, he toed off his boots and neatly put them on the boot tray. She did the same, then allowed him to help with removing her cloak and bonnet. "Hiya, Heart!" he called out. "Where are you?"

"I'm putting away towels in the linen closet. Daed, you're too early. Supper ain't for another hour."

"I know that. I came inside for a different reason." Leading Mary into the kitchen, Levi added, "Mary's here. She came for a visit. Come talk to her because she needs your help."

Mary felt like rolling her eyes. Not only was Levi acting as if she wasn't standing right in front of him, but he was making it sound as if she was the one who was sick. "You didn't need to make it sound like that, Levi."

"Like how?"

"Like it's urgent," she fired back in a whisper.

He blinked slowly. "It involves you, Jerry and Flora, a litter of puppies, and this house. I reckon that means it's pretty urgent indeed."

While she was pondering his words, Heart joined them. "Hiya, Mary. It's nice to see you here."

"It's *gut* to see you, too, dear. I hope I'm not disturbing you too much."

"Not at all. I was only putting away a load of towels. Supper is almost done. Please come in and sit down." She looked around. "Want to go sit in the dining room?"

"Thank you."

Leading Mary into the next room, Heart smiled at her father. "Thanks for getting me, Daed."

Instead of going back outside, Levi followed. "How come we have to wait an hour if supper is almost done?"

"Because we eat at five o'clock, Daed."

Mary was just about to tease Levi about his schedule when she noticed that Heart had on a sweater, too.

Hers was also blue . . . and Spike's tail was poking out of the kangaroo pocket on the front of it. "Heart, are you carrying Spike around the house?"

"Hmm? Oh, yes." She looked embarrassed, but pleased, as she pulled him out of her pocket and held him on her palm. "He seems to like being in this little pocket. The two of us have become *gut* friends."

"I guess you have." Sure that Levi would have a lot to say about a rat in the kitchen, Mary glanced his way.

To her surprise, Levi didn't look dismayed at all. If anything, he looked as if he was disappointed not to be holding Spike.

"I checked out a book from the library on fancy rats," Heart said. "I wanted to learn as much as I could about them. Rats are actually rather clean and orderly animals."

"I . . . did not know that."

"They're social, too. Just like you said. He didn't look too happy to be alone in his cage all day."

"I'm glad you are doing so well with him." Figuring Spike was a perfect segue, Mary added, "Actually, I came over to ask if you could help me out with another pet, Heart."

"I'd be happy to. What do you need?"

"I'm going to be caring for another patient starting tomorrow." Never forgetting that she had been at their house for Katie's last days, she tried to skim over the details. "He's not doing well. I won't be able to check on Virginia and her pups very often. Would you mind visiting them at least once a day?"

"Of course not. I'll be happy to help."

Pleased that Heart didn't seem to mind and that Levi was right there so she wouldn't have to worry about informing him as well, she grinned. "*Danke.* I'll be very grateful, and I know Virginia and the puppies will be glad not to be alone all day. Now, I brought a key—"

"*Nee,*" Levi interrupted.

Spirits sinking, Mary turned to him. "*Nee?*"

"I'm sorry, but I don't think Heart visiting Virginia at your house a couple of times a day is a *gut* idea."

Before Mary could ask him to explain himself, Heart sighed. "Daed, I'm not a little girl any longer. I think it's time you realized that I can and should be able to manage my own schedule."

"It might surprise you, but I'm aware that you are no longer a little girl helping me in the corner of my workshop." He looked Mary square in the eye. "What I'm trying to say is, I think the dogs should come live over here while you are watching Jerry. I think that's the best idea of all."

Mary was so shocked, she could've been knocked over with a feather. "Are you sure about this, Levi? I wouldn't have time to retrieve them every night."

"I know."

Darting a look at Heart, Mary tried to make sure both father and daughter understood that they might be watching the puppies for longer than anticipated. But how did she bring up the fact that Jerry was dying without reminding Heart of her mother's passing? "And . . . ah, there's no telling how long I might be at the Hochstetler *haus.*"

"Mary, I know you're dancing around the truth for

our sake, but it ain't necessary," Levi said in a rough tone. "I know the Lord is calling Jerry to Heaven, and I have a feeling Heart understands that, too."

"I guessed as much," Heart said. "The days you were here are a hazy blur, but I do remember that you slept in the guest bedroom . . . or didn't sleep at all. It was such a comfort knowing you were there."

The girl's words were humbling. To hear how her efforts had affected Heart made Mary feel validated. "Thank you for saying that. I'm sorry I was speaking in such a vague way. I didn't want to bring up bad memories."

"They're not all bad," Levi said, surprising her. "You made Katie as comfortable as she could be and gave Heart and me a feeling of peace." He cleared his throat. "That is why I think it's best if we look after the dogs."

"All right," she agreed with a smile. *"Danke."*

The back door opened and the sound of Clayton washing his hands and removing his boots could be heard in the kitchen. When he walked in, he drew up short. "Sorry, I didn't realize you had a guest."

"You're welcome to join us, Clayton," Heart said. "Guess what? We're going to be watching Virginia and the puppies!"

Clayton darted a look at her. "I see."

Levi chuckled. "I don't think you see at all, but that's okay. I'm sure Heart will fill you in when you go help her retrieve the puppies tonight."

"Do you mind helping me get them?" Heart asked.

"Of course not."

"Perhaps you should take the buggy," Levi said. "You can drive one, yes?"

"Yes."

"I can drive a buggy just fine," Heart said.

"Sure, but can you hold five squirming puppies at the same time?"

Mary put down her coffee cup. "Should we go now?"

"It's almost supper. Please stay," Heart said. "That is, if you don't mind. I made a chicken potpie and there's more than enough for one extra person."

It had been far too long since she'd had anything that sounded so good. "I would love to stay for supper. *Danke.*"

Levi smiled. "It's settled then. You'll stay for supper. Then the three of you can take the buggy to your *haus*, and Heart and Clayton can bring the pups back here."

Mary noticed that Levi had very neatly arranged it all so he didn't have to do anything. Noticing the looks Clayton and Heart exchanged, she realized she wasn't the only one to notice.

Heart stood up. "Mary, would you like to help me bring the serving dishes to the table?"

"Of course, dear."

"Heart, what about your rat?" Levi asked.

"Oh! I'd completely forgotten I was holding him. Here, Daed."

Looking on, Clayton laughed at the look on Levi's face.

They all did. Except for Spike.

The rat stared at him intently before walking up the man's arm. Just as if he'd done it before.

Once again, Mary realized that she didn't know Levi nearly as well as she'd thought. She also found that everything she was discovering she liked very much.

Very much indeed.

Chapter 21

It turned out that not a one of the six dogs was a fan of going for a buggy ride. Not a one of the five puppies, who were squirming and pawing at the sides of the wicker basket resting on Heart's lap. Not Virginia, who was sitting on the other side of her on the buggy's bench seat. The usually mellow golden retriever was tense and whining. Honestly, she was acting as if Heart and Clayton had dognapped her.

From the moment they left Mary's house, Heart had been in constant motion, trying to soothe Virginia and prevent the tiny pups from escaping.

Next to her, Clayton was looking like the very picture of a handsome Amish man. He was dressed in a knit cap, blue shirt, sweater, gray pants, and boots. His black wool coat was unbuttoned and opened. He was holding Becket's lines easily, his focus completely on the road and the horse.

As it should be.

She just wished it was on her instead.

As one of the puppies, the true escape artist, nipped at her finger and then let out a pitiful wail, Heart groaned. "Puppy, it's gonna be all right." Carefully repositioning him on the soft fleece blanket Mary had placed in the basket, she added, "Just relax. We'll be at my house soon."

He whined again, which made Virginia tense up and nudge Heart's side. "I mean you no harm, Virginia. Have a little bit of faith, *jah?*"

Clayton cast her a sideways glance. "I don't know if that's going to be possible, Heart."

She grunted. "I'm starting to regret letting you drive the buggy."

His lips twitched again. "Because you don't think I'm driving well or because it's the easier job?"

One of the pups tackled the others, making the basket shake. She gripped it harder. "Because it's easier, of course."

When all five of the puppies began barking in unison, he chuckled. "*Jah*, it surely is."

Realizing that she was complaining far too much, she giggled, too. "They are a handful, aren't they?"

"They are. But at least they're a cute handful."

"They surely are. And at least we're almost home."

"We are indeed." After another minute passed, and the pups miraculously stopped barking and whining, Clayton spoke again. "Hey, ah, Heart?"

"Jah?"

"That's quite a job Mary has. Does seeing her ever make you sad?" He waved a hand. "You know, because she lived at your *haus* when your *mamm* died?"

His question caught her off guard, but Heart forced herself to think about the answer. "You know what? *Nee.* A lot of people die suddenly or in the hospital. Because of Mary, Daed and I were blessed to have as much time with Mamm as we could."

Forcing herself to remember the details of her mother's last hours, she added, "Mary took care of a lot of things so that my father and I could focus on Mamm. Whenever I see her, I'm actually a little bit in awe of her. Her job ain't easy, but she takes it in stride."

"Have you noticed that she and your father seem to talk a lot?"

"What do you mean?"

"Oh, nothing. . . . It's, ah . . . I happened to notice that they seem to be on friendly terms."

"I noticed that as well." Repositioning a pup again, she added, "I'm so glad you said that. I thought I was the only one who thought there was something going on between them."

"Does it bother you?"

"Not really. It's out of my hands, anyway. I'm going to let the Lord figure that relationship out."

"I reckon that's the right approach."

"But, Clayton, I've been noticing my father look at her a lot. He softens his voice around her, too. And I've seen Mary blush around him." When he didn't say anything, she said, "Was there a reason you brought it up?"

"Not really. I was simply making conversation."

"Oh." While she couldn't deny that talking about a possible romance brewing between her father and Mary Miller was far more entertaining than listening to her complain about dogs, Heart couldn't help but be disappointed.

Mainly because she had kind of thought that she and Clayton were becoming close, too.

Clayton let out a long, drawn-out sigh. "Heart, I wasn't just making conversation. Should I tell you what I've really been thinking?"

"Yes." She stared at his profile. Noticed that a muscle in his jaw was clenched. There was obviously something on his mind. "I think we can discuss just about anything now, don't you?"

"Maybe."

"Clayton, just tell me!"

"Fine. I don't think that Levi is the only man at your house looking at a certain woman a little too long and maybe a little too intensely." Lowering his voice, he added, "As a matter of fact, I am fairly certain that there's a man in your life who can't seem to do much of anything when you're around." He groaned. "Even, it seems, make sense."

He was pulling into their drive. The puppies had at last settled down and Virginia had her eyes closed. They were completely alone. She could either say nothing or be brave, too.

"I don't think it's just the men in the house who might be doing things like that, Clayton." There. It wasn't exactly a proclamation, but it was something.

"Yeah?" He sounded pleased.

She nodded.

"So, then, maybe one day . . . we—"

"Do you need help getting out?" her father called.

And just like that, the moment ended. She opened the door. "*Jah*, Daed. Come get some puppies."

She couldn't help but smile when he didn't hesitate. "Ah, you tiny hunds. Look at you."

After giving her a wink, he picked up the basket and headed into the house. Virginia lifted her head and watched him, but didn't follow.

"Why don't you head on inside, too? It's cold. I'll take care of the buggy and Becket."

"All right." Feeling a little shy and unsettled, she climbed down and helped Virginia get down safely, too. As they walked to the house, Clayton led the horse and buggy into the barn. Waiting while Virginia did her business, she lifted her head, felt the cold air against her cheeks, and reminded herself that God didn't make mistakes. Whatever was happening between them was meant to be.

Heart believed that. She just wished He would give her a hint of what was in their future.

Chapter 22

It was three in the morning again. After tossing and turning for twenty minutes, Levi pulled on his sweatshirt and walked to the living room. Spike, who'd been playing with some kind of rubber cube, dropped it and went to the cage's door.

"This has become our time together, hasn't it, rat?" he asked as he opened the door and gently cradled the animal in his palm.

Just as he was about to sit down on the couch, as he usually did, he spied the red tablecloth. Maybe it was time to sit in the dining room with his memories for a change.

Pulling out one of the side chairs, he took a seat, realizing belatedly that he'd subconsciously chosen the place where Katie had always sat. Hmm.

Now used to Spike's habits, he placed the rat on his lap. Spike liked to crawl to the edge of his sweatshirt and curl up. Levi barely noticed his movements.

What had happened with that tablecloth? Why had he gotten so upset about seeing this particular Christmas memory?

And what had led him not only to ache to help Mary as she watched over Jerry and Flora, but volunteer to watch Virginia and her litter of puppies?

"Katie, have you been keeping watch over me of late? Are you trying to tell me something?"

He didn't expect a reply, but he wished she would give him a sign. But . . . maybe she had.

Running a finger along the embroidery, he let his mind drift back to other Decembers. Other months when there'd been less snow and more activity.

Katie had made the whole month special: Christmas cards, baked goods, pine-scented candles, wrapped presents.

And a bright red tablecloth honoring her family and adding a splash of color to an otherwise very Plain house. Then, after she'd passed, he had ruthlessly created a rather gray world for both Heart and him. He'd worked more and more, spending almost every waking hour either at his forge or in his workshop. Along the way he'd begun to expect just as much from Heart.

Heart, who'd lost her mother and had to be grieving, had done everything he asked.

And he had asked for so much. She'd cooked and cleaned, did laundry and took care of the hens. She'd served him three meals a day at exactly the moment he'd asked them to be served. She'd given up going to gatherings of her friends or expecting too much free time. She'd just given and given and given.

And he had acted as if it was too much trouble to take off his boots so she wouldn't have to sweep the kitchen floor again.

He was so ashamed.

"You added brightness to my world, Katie," he said out loud. "And when you left, instead of searching for brightness in other places, I tamped it out. That wasn't right."

When Spike squeaked, Levi picked him up again. And, because Heart wasn't around to see, let him stand on the tablecloth. The rat's head turned right and left and then right again. Levi couldn't help but be amused; Spike, no doubt, wondered how he'd arrived at such a very red and fancy spot. He nudged the embroidery with his nose.

"Don't gnaw on the stitches, Spike."

The rat wiggled his whiskers, just as if he was offended by the thought. And then he walked back to Levi's hand.

"*Jah*, I suppose that cloth ain't all that good for exploring. Maybe you're tired, too, *jah?*" He stood up and returned the rat to his cage.

Paused when he heard a faint yip from one of the puppies, who were all in Heart's room with her.

"Dogs and a rat and Clayton. We have a houseful, Katie. I'm not sure what happened, but it all did."

Suddenly it occurred to him—he'd finally let down his guard. Though he no longer had Katie, he'd found joy and comfort in other ways, such as having an apprentice who also needed a home.

In watching a litter of messy, noisy, needy puppies so someone else could do God's work.

And even finding something special about an unwanted rat. For seeing his value and accepting it.

Finally he'd allowed Heart to be Heart. She was decorating and arguing with him and planning her future . . . and maybe even falling for a very good man, who obviously thought she was special.

"*Danke*, Katie," he said as he crawled back into bed. "Thank you for helping me bring brightness back into, my life. I promise I won't let you down again."

Just after nine o'clock the following morning, the door of his workshop burst open. Levi was so startled, he dropped the horseshoe he was making on the ground. It fell with a clang and a parade of sparks.

Clayton had barely jumped out of the way in time.

"Daed, I need you!" Heart said.

He tossed his steel tongs on a grate and rushed to her side. "What happened? Are you hurt?"

"*Nee.* The puppies are on the loose!"

Clayton, who had looked as if he'd been two seconds away from pulling Heart into his arms, gaped at her. "That's what's wrong?"

She scowled at them both. "Oh, don't either of you dare act as if I'm overreacting. Come help me round them up."

Levi loved his darling daughter, he truly did. But

there was no way he was running back to the house just to round up a couple of fluffy pups. "We're busy here, Heart."

"Oh, *nee*. You're not that busy." Popping both of her hands on her hips, she cleared her throat. "One of us volunteered to watch these dogs. All. The. Time."

Clayton, who'd gotten rather cheeky of late, chuckled. "I fear she has a point, Levi. You did offer to watch the dogs."

"Go on, then. Go help my daughter."

"Me?"

"You're the apprentice."

Clayton looked prepared to argue, then seemed to think better of it. "All right."

"*Nee*, Clayton. Daed, you are going to help us, too. The tiny tornadoes are destroying everything in sight, including your new slippers."

"Heart, I really like those slippers."

"Furthermore, what they aren't trying to destroy, they are pooping on."

"Well, if there's, ah, poop involved, I guess I should help."

"We need to hurry. They've been alone this whole time. They're probably tearing open all the Christmas presents I just wrapped."

Clayton curved a hand around her shoulders. "Let's go save Christmas, Heart." Shooting Levi a meaningful look over his shoulder, he added, "I'm sure your father will be along in a moment."

Heart moved to follow Clayton, but before she walked out of sight, she sent a look back at him. "You better join us, Daed," she warned. "Otherwise you're going to get to figure out your supper all on your own."

His formerly mild-mannered daughter had just delivered an ultimatum. Levi counted to five, giving Clayton a moment to try to calm Heart down, then followed them into the house.

When he arrived, he realized that Heart had not lied. A floor lamp had been knocked down. There was a hole chewed in his favorite blanket. And . . . yes . . . the telltale signs of un–potty-trained puppies littered the floor.

And that was only what he saw in the first five minutes.

Just as he was about to call out to Heart, a wayward pup ran toward him with a tiny yip. He bent down and scooped it up. "I have one!" he called.

"Three others are contained!" Clayton called.

"Ah, that leaves one. Where is it?"

"I think it's hiding in your room, Daed," Heart said.

"My room?" Handing the puppy in his hand to Heart, he strode to his bedroom, and then at last discovered the puppy lying on his bathroom floor . . . happily chewing on a sock.

Bending down, he pulled on the sock, but the puppy growled and tugged back.

Levi wanted to be annoyed. He really did. He had work to do and an upset daughter to placate. But when the pup tugged on the sock again, he couldn't help but give the other end a little tug back.

Pleased, the dog yipped happily and wagged its tail. He grinned . . . just as he noticed a ray of light shining down through his bathroom window. Bright and clear. Reminding him of his middle-of-the-night conversation with his wife.

"I see it, Katie," he whispered. "Clear as day, too. And, *jah*, I agree. It's time to keep moving forward and embrace the changes. Once and for all."

"Daed?"

"In here, child."

"Did you find . . . Oh!" She frowned. "Are you seriously sitting on the bathroom floor playing with this little fiend?"

"I'm afraid so, dear. He's awfully cute."

"It's a girl dog, Daed. A sneaky, sock-destroying girl puppy."

He smiled at her. "She's not so bad. Just a little lively." Reaching down, he picked her up—and her new toy, his sock. "I'll put her back in the pen." As he walked by, he pressed his lips to Heart's brow. "Relax, daughter. Everything is going to be just fine. I'm sure of it."

He grinned when he spied her skeptical look. Yes, everything in their house was in disarray, but at the moment he didn't want to change a thing.

Chapter 23

If Garrett had told Clayton how varied his duties would be at Levi Beachy's farm, he would've thought his mentor was lying. Living in the children's home, he was used to hard work. He was accustomed to sweeping dust and shoveling snow and pruning bushes. He was used to pitching in, in the kitchen. He'd even learned a thing or two about doing laundry and washing bathrooms.

But he'd never imagined being asked to perform his current chore: puppy duty. To be fair, Levi wasn't the one who'd asked him to watch the puppies.

It had all started the night before at supper. When they were almost done eating a delicious meal of meat loaf, mashed potatoes, peas and carrots, and fresh bread, Heart had asked him and her father if they could possi-

bly watch the puppies for a spell. Some ladies had invited
her to a coffee-and-Christmas-cookie party. It seemed
the ladies each brought a couple of dozen cookies, visited together and had lunch, then shared them all. She
promised she'd return with a mixture of at least three
dozen cookies.

Clayton hadn't known how to respond. Heart's expression had been so full of hope and excitement, he
sure hadn't wanted to be the person to tell her no. But it
also hadn't been up to him.

So instead of volunteering to help, he'd looked at
Levi first. A myriad of emotions had appeared on the
man's face, uppermost a sweet look of tenderness.
Then he'd nodded.

"Of course, Heart."

"Truly? You wouldn't mind?"

"Of course not. All day long you cook and clean for
Clayton and me. Now you're watching puppies for
Mary, even though having them here was my idea in
the first place. There's no way I'm going to deny you
this bit of enjoyment."

Feeling he should add something, Clayton said,
"Besides, think of all the cookies you'll bring home.
We're all going to enjoy those."

Heart exhaled, breathing a sigh of relief. "Thank
you so much. Daed, after supper I'll show you what
to do."

"Do?" Levi asked.

Heart nodded. "I've got them on a schedule, you
see. It won't take long."

"Tell Clayton, child. Not me."

"Pardon?" Clayton asked.

"You don't think I'm going to chase after five balls of fluff if I have you, do you?"

"Well, ah . . ." He made the mistake of looking at Heart. Her eyes were wide and she was worrying her bottom lip. "No." Because . . . what else could he say?

"That settles it," Levi said as he stood up. "You may help Heart with the dishes and then learn about the puppies' schedule for tomorrow."

"What about your schedule? Do you need me to write tomorrow's appointments down for you?"

"Of course not. I managed just fine before you ever came along, pup," he said as he carried his plate to the kitchen. "I'll be fine tomorrow. Heart?"

She got to her feet and faced him. "Yes, Daed?"

"I enjoyed your supper. Thank you." He walked over, kissed her brow, and then walked to his bedroom and closed the door. Feeling rather foolish, he stared at the closed door.

"Do you think your father is staying in there for the rest of the night?" Clayton asked.

"It's only six o'clock. No." Folding her arms over her chest, Heart stared at the closed door. "Daed went in there so he wouldn't have to help with the dishes or hear about the puppies' needs. If he was here and you had a problem, he'd feel obligated to help, you see."

"I don't know what to think about that."

"Oh, I do." Her lips pursed before she shrugged. Turning to him, she smiled. "Oh, well. There are some things I'd like to change and some things I know just aren't worth the effort. This is one of those."

Clayton didn't disagree. So, instead of commenting on Levi's behavior, he walked to the table and picked up their dishes. "Would you like to wash or dry?"

"Are you really offering me a choice?"

"Yes. I've washed my fair share of dishes."

"In that case, I'll dry."

He had a feeling she chose that job on purpose, just to see him squirm. But he had a surprise for her. He didn't mind doing dishes at all. Squirting soap into the sink, he rolled up his sleeves and got to work.

With both of them working together, the kitchen was clean in no time. He'd also gotten the opportunity to tease her a bit about her dress, which was a dark shade of cranberry. The fabric was a soft wool and she had on thick socks, but no shoes. He'd thought she looked especially fetching. But instead of telling her that, he'd merely accused her of dressing for Christmas almost a week too early.

By the time they walked into the living room and she released Spike, who'd been happily gnawing on some kind of hard biscuit, Heart was once again relaxed and happy.

"Are you ready to hear about what to do?"

"Of course."

"Okay. First thing you'll need to do is count the puppies."

"Excuse me?"

"A couple of them get a little too rambunctious. If

you're not careful, one out of the five will sneak off and get into trouble."

"I'll do my best to keep track of all five."

"I'm serious, Clayton."

"I am taking you seriously. Anything else?"

"Yes." She told him all about cleaning the papers in the pen, about how to dispose of the soiled papers, and how to bathe any of the puppies who accidentally stepped, rolled, or wandered into other dogs' messes. Then she told him about feeding time, since the puppies were getting weaned and were now eating a small amount of puppy food.

By the time she finished, Clayton was wishing he'd taken notes. "How long will you be gone, do you think?"

"I'm not exactly sure. Maybe four hours?"

"Four hours?"

"Well, yes. It's a party and lunch. Is four hours too long for you?"

Yes. Yes, it was. *"Nee."*

"Are you sure?" She glanced at her father's closed door. "Do you want me to ask Daed to come out? I could tell him that he has to help you, too."

"Nee. Don't do that."

"But—"

"I was taken by surprise. I'll be fine."

Little by little, her look of doubt changed into happiness. "I'm so excited about tomorrow. I made buckeyes to take."

He looked around. "Where are they?"

"In the outside refrigerator."

"Are there any extras for me and your *daed?*"

"Not tonight. I'll give you one tomorrow. If there are any left over."

Clayton was fairly sure there wouldn't be. Heart was such a fantastic cook, he had a feeling her cookies were going to be everyone's favorite.

By the time he'd been watching the puppies for two hours the next day, Clayton was sure that not even a platter of buckeyes would make up for the pain and suffering those five puppies had caused him. They cried and played, ate and made messes. In short, they did everything five puppies were supposed to do. He'd almost been prepared for that.

What he hadn't been prepared for was the way they'd gotten together and launched an escape. Honestly, one minute he'd been throwing away old newspapers and refilling a water bowl, and the next they'd scattered like an overturned bag of marbles.

"Nee!" he'd said. As if they'd ever listen.

They assuredly did not. They ignored him and ran every which way. Going under the coffee table, and the couch, and Levi's favorite easy chair. Every time he captured one and put it in the pen, the pup would cry and yip pitifully. And then, somehow, immediately develop a plot to escape again.

After ten minutes—which felt like a whole day's work next to a forge—he'd developed a sweat.

He needed help.

"Virginia, some help here, please."

The dog, who'd been asleep on the couch, merely opened one eye and then closed it again. Just beyond her, safe from harm's way, was Spike. The rat was staring at Clayton with a combination of interest and disdain.

Clayton didn't blame him for that. No doubt the rodent was thinking he was as dumb as he looked.

Fifteen minutes later, he had four out of five puppies back in their pen and they were asleep. That was the good news.

The bad news was one was still on the loose. He'd looked everywhere in the living room. Walking into the hall, he was glad that Heart had reminded him to keep all the doors shut. That left the kitchen and dining area.

Grumbling to himself, he looked high and low, but with no luck. Beginning to get concerned, he looked half-heartedly in the mudroom.

And found the missing pup.

"Aha!" he cried, scaring the little thing. She let out a fierce bark.

Which made her release the item that had been keeping her content and out of sight: one of Heart's black boots.

"What have you done?" he whispered. He wasn't talking to the puppy, either. He was talking to himself. Because the boot's top had been chewed well and good. The leather was ruined. The lace was bitten in half.

Feeling rather sick, he carried the wayward pup

back to the pen and then fetched the damaged boot. What was he going to tell Heart?

The woman had three pairs of shoes: her henhouse/outside-work tennis shoes, her church/company boots, which were on her feet, and then these. Her favorites. She made a point of always keeping them neatly put away and had even told him once that they were the most expensive pair of boots she'd ever owned. The leather was buttery soft and the craftsmanship was evident. Heart said they fit her like a glove and that the man at the store said they'd last for years if they were taken care of. She was right to be fond of them.

Standing back in the living room, he turned the boot over in his hands, wondering if there was a way to mend the tattered leather.

"What now?" he asked himself.

The door opened.

"Clayton?"

It was Levi. The purchaser of the boot. Panic hit him hard. Maybe he lost his mind for a second, too? There was no other explanation for why he opened a deep drawer behind him and stuffed that boot far back into it. Behind a Yahtzee game and an old crochet throw.

"Yes?"

"What is for lunch?"

"I don't know," he said.

Stomping into the kitchen, leaving a trail of snow, Levi stared at him. "You didn't make anything?"

"*Nee.* I've been pretty busy with the dogs."

Only then did Clayton realize what Levi must be

seeing: one caged rat, one sleeping dog on the couch, and five sleeping puppies in a pen.

"I can see that," Levi said. In a very sarcastic tone.

Clayton glanced at the clock. He had one more hour to go before Heart came home. One more hour to figure out what to do about the damaged boot.

For the first time all day, he sincerely hoped she ran late.

Chapter 24

She needed to get out of the house more often. The party had been so much fun! All the women had been in good spirits and had lots of stories to tell. Some, like Addie Schott and May Hilty, wore blushes as the older ladies teased them about newlywed life.

Other women good-naturedly complained about being tired, describing their days filled with housework and toddlers. A few others talked about shopping trips they'd taken, trips planned, and the number of Christmas cards they sent out.

In the middle of it all was Lavinia Stutzman, Addie's grandmother. She had something to say about everything. Even Heart's father's new apprentice.

"He's a right fine-looking man, Heart," she'd announced with a cackle. "You'd do far worse than to catch him."

Though Heart agreed, she knew better than to say a thing. All eyes would be on her and knowing glances would be exchanged. That was the problem with being one of the only single women in the room. Every other woman was ready to play matchmaker.

Lavinia's nosey questions aside, by the time Heart walked home with a container holding four dozen assorted Christmas cookies, her spirit had been lifted. She'd needed the company of other women and was beyond grateful to live in such a close and loving community. Some of Clayton's stories about his childhood had made her realize how much she'd taken her life for granted. Yes, she'd lost her mother too early, and she did live a rather solitary existence, but it was a good life.

Plus, she now had Spike. And maybe, one day, Clayton Glick as well.

"Heart Glick," she whispered to herself. "Hi, I'm Heart. Heart Glick." Even though the air around her was frosty, she was sure her cheeks were bright red. What a silly girl she'd become, dreaming about strong, handsome, dark-haired Clayton and his caramel-colored eyes and kind nature.

When she spied her house and barn, she reminded herself that she had a great many other things to do besides daydream about weddings, proposals, and new last names. She had supper to prepare, a house to clean, and a bunch of dogs and a rat to take care of.

"At least Christmas is coming," she whispered to herself. She'd be able to take a whole day of rest then.

"Hello!" she called out when she opened the door. "Clayton, are you here?"

"*Jah.* I'm in with the puppies."

Taking care to remove her church boots, she hurried through the kitchen and into the living room. Clayton was sitting on the floor with two of the puppies. To her amazement, Spike was sitting on his shoulder.

"Clayton, look at you!"

Meeting her eyes, he grinned. "What? Are you most impressed by the clean living room, the puppies, or the rat on my shoulder?"

"All of it." Walking closer, she said, "I'm a little embarrassed. I was half expecting to walk in and find dishes in the sink, trash on the floor, and multiple messes to clean up."

He stood up and deposited two puppies back in their pen. "I'm a little offended. Did you really think I'd do such a poor job in your absence?"

"*Nee.*" Maybe.

His gaze warmed. "I'm pleased I surprised you, then." When Spike squeaked, Clayton laughed. "Want to rescue your rodent?"

"Of course." She retrieved Spike and held him carefully in her hands. Shook her head slightly. "Could you give me a few minutes? I want to change out of this dress and into an older gray one."

"Of course. You look pretty in blue, though. I don't know if I told you that."

It was vain, but she'd chosen the fabric because it

was almost the exact shade of her eyes. She might have chosen to wear it in the hopes that Clayton would notice. Now that he had, she felt flustered. "*Danke*, Clayton. I'll be right back." She hurried to her room, carefully depositing Spike on her bed, while she removed pins, hung up her dress, and then pulled on a dark gray one and pinned it again.

All the while Spike watched. When she was dressed again, she picked him up and kissed his tiny head. "You are a blessing to me, Spike." When he tilted his head to one side, Heart couldn't help but smile.

Suddenly remembering that she was in stocking feet, she hurried back out. She needed to put on her favorite boots so she could get to work. Clayton was standing in the kitchen, drinking a cup of coffee.

"Want a cup, Heart? It's fresh."

"Maybe in a little bit. I'm going to put on my boots and start on supper first."

"Why are you putting on boots to cook?"

Realizing she still held on to Spike, she placed him in his cage, but left the door open so he could leave if he wanted. "You know why," she replied. "It's cold outside and the wood floors don't feel all that good against stocking feet."

"Want me to get them for you?"

"Nee." Feeling a little concerned, she gave him a long look as she walked past him again. "Are you okay?"

"Of course. Why?"

"Because you're kind of acting like something's wrong," she said as she picked up a boot. "Did something happen with Daed today?"

"Nope."

"Are you sure?" Realizing that the mate wasn't next to the boot, she picked up the boots she'd worn to the party and looked underneath them.

"Positive. Your father and I even made our own lunch today," he added.

"Hmm." She got to her feet and looked around the area. Where was the right boot? "Hey, Clayton?"

"Yeah?"

"Ah, have you seen the mate to this boot?"

He shook his head. *"Nee."*

"Are you sure?"

"Heart, I don't really spend much time in this room, beyond washing my hands and taking off my own shoes."

"You're right."

"What's wrong? Did you misplace one of your boots?"

"I guess I did." It didn't make sense, though. She held up the left boot. "I don't understand why I have one boot, but not the other. This is the strangest thing."

"It is . . . unless you're Cinderella."

She dropped the boot on the floor. "What?"

"Sorry. I just happened to see the broom in the corner and thought about you having a missing shoe."

She remembered hearing the story when she was a little girl. A pretty orphan named Cinderella had to cook and clean, and was ignored by mean relatives. She talked to mice and horses and birds. When she went to a ball and met Prince Charming, she lost a glass slipper.

"I'm not Cinderella."

His eyes widened. "Of course, you ain't. I'm going to the barn to see your father." Pulling his coat off the hook and slipping a knit cap over his head, he strode out the door.

When it slammed behind him, Heart picked up all the shoes and arranged them again. Looked in corners, then spied the broom. She certainly was sweeping a lot. She also talked to a rat. And now she had a missing boot.

The comparison was fanciful and silly. After all, she had no fairy godmother and no Prince Charming.

"God, I don't know where you're going with this, but I hope you finish this lesson real soon. It's getting a bit too odd for me."

Putting on her old tennis shoes, she got to work. Later, she'd search her room. Her missing boot had to be somewhere.

It couldn't have simply vanished . . . could it?

Chapter 25

Mary was tired. So tired. She'd spent much of the last twenty-four hours with Jerry and Flora. As Jerry had gotten weaker and weaker, Mary had administered the medicine the traveling nurse had left and tried to keep him comfortable. Whenever he'd fallen asleep, she'd tried to comfort Flora as best she could.

Mary knew how hard it was to watch someone fight for his life. She also had been at bedsides where the patient was more than ready to go to Heaven. Not a bit of it was easy for loved ones to watch.

Some handled it better than others. Mary didn't know why that was. She did believe, however, that all people grieved in their own ways. Neither tears nor fervent prayers gave a true account of how a person felt on the inside. Levi Beachy had surely been an example of that.

When she'd been with Katie during her last days, Mary had sometimes assumed that Levi wasn't feeling much. Of course, she'd eventually realized that hadn't been the case at all. He simply wasn't the type of man to show emotion.

Flora, on the other hand, was the complete opposite. She'd either been crying nonstop or wanted to tell stories about her beloved husband to whoever would listen.

Mary had been happy to do whatever she could do. She truly did feel sorry for Flora. But that didn't mean she didn't need a break. When Jerry's extended family arrived, one of his *English* nephews, Peter, volunteered to drive her home.

When the young man approached the Beachy farm, she made a sudden decision. "Drop me off here, would you, please?"

"Sure thing, Mary."

When he drew to a stop next to the house, she saw two kerosene lanterns glowing through the windows. The family was home. "Thank you so much."

"Thank you for taking such good care of Uncle Jerry and Aunt Flora."

She smiled tiredly as she got out. "It's my honor, Peter. You take care now."

"Will you need a ride in the morning?"

"Thank you, but no." It was only about a forty-minute walk to Jerry and Flora's house. Since the weather was supposed to be clear, she was looking forward to the exercise. Sitting bedside for hours on end was hard on her body.

The front door opened just as Peter drove away. Turning, she saw Levi.

"Hi."

"Hiya," he said, his careful gaze seeming to take in every inch of her—from her bloodshot eyes to her wrinkled gray dress peeking out from under her black cloak. "I didn't expect to see ya this evening."

"I wasn't planning to stop by." Suddenly realizing that she was assuming he wouldn't mind, she added, "I was hoping I could see the puppies for a little bit. Would you mind?"

"Of course not." He opened the door wider. "Come inside. Have you eaten?"

"Supper?"

"*Jah*, Mary."

She tried to remember the last time she'd eaten. It had been hours ago. "I don't think so."

"*Ach*, Mary." He held out his hands for her cloak and bonnet. "Give me your things and come inside by the fireplace. I'll heat up some leftovers from supper."

"Do you have food to spare?"

He nodded. "Heart had a busy day, so we had soup and sandwiches. There's plenty for you."

"*Danke.*" The warm food sounded almost as good as not having to make it. "I'll take off my boots and join you in the living room."

"I'm glad you came over. You shouldn't be alone right now."

Mary figured she should point out that she wasn't Flora, and therefore had nothing to complain about, but the truth of the matter was that she was emotionally drained. She loved her job, but it wasn't always easy. Today it had all caught up with her.

Walking into the living room, she noticed that both Heart and Clayton were on the floor near the pen, and three of the puppies were playing with them. The other two were sleeping next to Virginia. When Virginia saw her, she wagged her tail.

"Hi, Mary," Heart called out. "It's good to see ya."

"You too." After she exchanged greetings with Clayton, she sat down on the couch. "I decided to stop by on my way home."

"I'm glad you did." Lowering her voice, Heart added, "*Mei daed* said that he was going to make you a sandwich and heat up your soup."

"Isn't that something?" she whispered.

Her eyes filled with mischief, Heart nodded. "He's doing all kinds of things today. He even fixed his own lunch."

"I heard that!" Levi called out. "Heart, you are getting a bit cheeky. I'll have you know that I've always been able to make a sandwich and work the oven."

"Yes, Daed." When it looked like she was going to add something else, Clayton shook his head.

"*Nee*, Heart," he murmured. "No reason to point out what we all know is the truth, *jah?*"

Right in front of Mary's eyes the young woman closed her mouth. Everything in Heart's expression softened. "All right, Clayton."

So . . . that *was* happening. Heart and Clayton were falling in love. Right in front of her eyes. They might not realize it, but she sure did. She used to look at Paul the same way.

And . . . maybe she sometimes felt that same pull toward Levi these days?

"Here you go, Mary," Levi said. "I'll bring your food to the table for ya."

"Danke."

Walking to the dining room, she found a thick sandwich cut neatly in half and a steaming bowl of chicken noodle soup. "This looks so good. A lot, but good."

To her surprise, Levi pulled out the chair across from her. He didn't speak until she finished giving silent thanks.

"If you can't finish your sandwich, you can take half of it home with ya."

"I'll appreciate that." Dipping her spoon into the soup, she said, "Tell me about your day."

"Oh, it weren't too busy. Nothing out of the ordinary, really. Nothing like the day Heart and Clayton had."

She swallowed her spoonful, then ladled up another one. "Oh?"

"Heart had a Christmas cookie party, so Clayton pet-sat."

"I trust she had a good time?"

"Heart, Mary asked if you had a good time," he called out.

"I did!"

Mary covered her mouth while she chewed her first bite of the massive sandwich. "And Clayton? How did he do with the puppies?"

"Clayton, how was watching the puppies?" Levi called out again.

"Exhausting!"

This was becoming ridiculous. "Levi, you don't have to call out my questions. You can answer me."

"Ain't no reason to do that if they're in the next room."

She supposed he had a point. "How about if just the two of us talk instead?"

"You've got to eat, Mary."

"Then it looks like the conversation is going to have to rely on you. Tell me something interesting."

"Hmm. Well, we do happen to have a bit of a mystery going on."

"What?" she asked after she swallowed another bite of her sandwich.

"It seems we have a missing boot." His bright eyes belied the somewhat-insignificant news.

She raised her eyebrows. "Is that right? Tell me all about it."

He lowered his voice. "It seems that at some time between yesterday and this afternoon, one of Heart's favorite boots vanished. It's created quite an uproar."

"Really?"

"Oh, *jah*. Heart is beside herself. She's looked all over the house. Actually, she's had all of us looking for the missing footwear."

"But so far, no luck?"

"Not a bit. I even looked in my closet—though why one of my daughter's boots would suddenly appear there, I have no idea."

"Hmm."

"Jah." He leaned back. "It's a mystery."

Bemused by the silly conversation, she leaned forward. "What do you think happened?"

"I couldn't say, though I know I didn't touch it. I never noticed Heart kept her best boots by the back door."

"Best boots?"

"That's what she calls them," he explained as she finished off half of the sandwich. "Furthermore, I know Spike couldn't have had anything to do with it."

"I would have to agree. Spike might make a nest in a boot, but taking it is beyond his capabilities."

"That means, either Heart misplaced the thing—"

"Which I rather doubt."

Levi nodded. "Or Clayton had something to do with the disappearance."

"Or one of the dogs," Mary mused. If there really was a missing "best boot," then she had a very strong hunch that one of the puppies was behind the mystery.

"Yes, or one of the dogs." His lips twitched. "Unfortunately, they aren't talking."

She chuckled. "I imagine not, especially if they know that sweet Heart is in a bit of a tizzy about it."

"Oh, she is."

Realizing that all of her soup was gone and her

stomach was full, Mary smiled at Levi. "I'm so glad I came by. Somehow you managed to fill my belly and lift my spirits all at the same time."

"I'm glad you came by, too. When you're ready, I'll take you home."

"*Danke*, Levi. I'll appreciate that."

The smile they shared was perfect.

Chapter 26

Two days had passed since Heart's boot had disappeared. *No, since you hid it in the drawer,* Clayton told himself silently.

What a mistake that had been. He never should have tried to hide the thing. He should have simply shown both Heart and his boss what had happened under his watch and offered to buy her a new pair of boots.

Sure, Heart might be upset with him, and Levi might think that he couldn't be trusted, and he might be missing a good chunk of money for a while, but at least it would all be out in the open.

Now, when Heart did learn the truth, she would think that he was a liar.

She would be right, too.

In his defense, he'd assumed that she would've forgotten about that blasted missing boot by now. She had two other sets of shoes, and with Christmas just a couple of days away, she had a lot of other things on her mind.

He'd been wrong, though. Not only had Heart not forgotten about the boot, she seemed to dwell on the mystery. He hadn't realized Heart could get so flustered and short-tempered.

After rather half-heartedly attempting to look for the boot, Levi had retreated to the barn. Clayton had decided to follow his lead and put in extra hours, too. To his surprise, all that extra time in the workshop had led to something of a silver lining: He and Levi had become friends and his skills were improving.

It was almost peaceful in the workshop. Levi Beachy was a man of habit and as methodical as a middle-school science teacher. As scattered and oblivious as he might be around the house, he was meticulous while working. Never did Step 4 follow anything but Step 3. *Never.*

Because of that, Clayton always knew what to expect. It seemed that the customers knew it, too. Men arrived on time, stayed with their horses, and paid promptly. Even the *English* clients, some who pulled in with rented vehicles or a hired crew to carry and secure a large piece of art, were respectful of Levi's time and talents.

Clayton had even commented on the phenomenon to a customer. A wealthy industrialist from Pittsburgh had responded with some cryptic words: "No one messes with Levi Beachy. Everyone knows he doesn't suffer fools."

So, though Clayton knew he did not have the same effect on other people, he had gotten used to the fact that there were few surprises.

Until today.

First the fire in the forge had acted sluggish; then one of Levi's best customers—a rancher with a dozen horses—had arrived over an hour late. It seemed everything had gone wrong.

Clayton had tried to please his boss by shoeing the horses and assisting with the forge and cleaning stalls. However, he wasn't sure if his efforts were making much of a difference or not. Levi got crankier and crankier—even going so far as to snap at Heart when she came out to let them know that their midday meal was ready and on the table.

When she'd turned away in a rush, obviously near tears, Clayton had wanted to run after her, but there was no time. An art customer had arrived, and hadn't been pleased with her sculpture. She'd shown Levi and Clayton pictures of the preliminary drawings and proclaimed that the finished product was too different.

Though Clayton didn't like her attitude, he had to admit that she was right. It was just a shame that the finished piece was far more beautiful than what she'd asked for.

And then Levi had gone and told her that.

Unfortunately, the customer had taken off in a huff, nearly getting in an accident with a horse trailer.

Watching the near accident from the doorway of the barn, Clayton prayed for strength. "This day."

"It's a bad one," Levi muttered behind him. He turned away toward the forge.

"I'll take care of the horse and Mr."—he looked at the neatly written schedule—"Jeffreys."

When Levi simply grunted, Clayton hoped the man would keep his bad mood to himself. He strode to the parking lot, where Mr. Jeffreys was already opening the back door of the horse trailer. "Mr. Jeffreys?"

"No one calls me that. I'm Alan."

"Alan, my name is Clayton. I'm Levi's apprentice."

Alan grinned as he directed the horse to back out of the trailer. "I hear you're a good bit more than that, Clay. Your reputation has preceded you."

That was a surprise, but it was good to hear. He was slowly coming into his own. He'd gone from being in awe, and half afraid of Levi, to simply hoping that he didn't mess up, to feeling more confident every day. He looked at the schedule again. "I understand we need new shoes for Buck."

Alan patted the palomino's side as the docile horse pawed the ground. "You understand, right?"

"Follow me to the barn. I have some horseshoes ready. We'll see how they fit."

"Good enough." He looked around. "Is Levi around?"

"Yes, sir. He's near the forge. Don't worry. He'll look over everything before you take Buck home."

"Good to know."

Just as they walked into the side door of the barn, Clayton caught another glimpse of Heart. She was standing on the front porch of the house. She was wearing her cape and sipping from a mug. When she looked his way, he raised a hand. But either she didn't see him or was upset, because she didn't respond.

Alan turned to see whom Clayton had waved to and smiled. "I always thought the Lord knew what He was doing when He gave such a pretty girl a man like Levi for a father."

"Oh?"

"If she had a weaker man for a father, every fellow in the county would likely be pestering her." He smiled, obviously showing that he meant his words as a compliment.

While he agreed that Heart was beautiful, Clayton didn't care for the idea of other men wanting her attention. He sure hoped Alan Jeffreys wasn't putting himself in the same group, but shook off his worry. "If you'd like to tie up Buck right here, I'll go get the shoes."

"That's fine. Take your time."

Just as he turned to go in, a clatter and a hoarse cry arose from the forge.

Clayton knew the scream had to be from Levi, but he was so accustomed to the man doing everything with ease, it was hard to believe what he'd heard.

Alarmed, he ran inside, barely aware of Alan on his heels.

The sight before them made his breath catch.

Levi was standing, but it looked as if he was still on two feet out of sheer will. He was holding his left arm tightly against his body, and it was obvious he was in extreme pain. Next to him was a block of steel. It was still red from the fire.

Rushing to his side, Clayton tried to determine whether the man was suffering a burn or something different. "Levi?" he called out.

Levi raised his chin slightly, but his gaze was unfocused.

"It's me," he said. When the man didn't respond, he added, "Clayton. Alan's here, too. What do you need? Should we call for the ambulance?"

"Hurt," Levi muttered through clenched teeth . . . just before he passed out.

Clayton barely made it to his side before his boss hit the floor. And that's when he saw it. It looked as if Levi's arm was broken. Now that he was unconscious, his arm was hanging at an awkward angle. Just as worrisome was the horrible cut and burn on his forearm. It looked as if the hot steel had not only cut through the skin, but seared the flesh around the wound. As blood began to seep down Levi's arm, Clayton had to force himself not to look away.

"Clayton?" Alan asked from behind him. "What's going on?"

Feeling as if he was in a fog, Clayton said, "Levi's had a bad accident. He passed out. We're going to need some help."

"This is bad," Alan said as he pulled out his phone and punched in numbers. "We're going to need an ambulance."

Thanking the Lord for Alan's presence, Clayton kept an eye on Levi. Remembering how he'd once helped a younger boy at the home by keeping his hand on his arm while he received stitches, Clayton stayed by Levi's side with his arm on the man's thick shoulders.

"They're on their way," Alan said, covering up the mouthpiece with his hand. "The dispatcher wants to know how he's doing?"

"He's still passed out."

"But he's breathing, right?"

"Yes." He swallowed. "I mean, I believe so." He pressed two fingers to the artery in Levi's neck. When he felt a pulse, he shuddered in relief. "He's alive."

"He's unconscious, but seems stable," Alan said into the receiver. "Hmm? Yeah. Okay. Thanks." Looking at Clayton, he said, "Maybe ten minutes out."

"Okay." Ten minutes felt like an eternity, but, of course, it wasn't. All they had to do was sit tight and wait. And pray. But as he closed his eyes to do just that, he realized what he'd forgotten.

Heart!

She was likely back in the house. Likely fuming about the fact that she'd made a meal neither of them had taken the time to eat. He knew her father was everything to her. He was all she had left.

He turned to the *Englischer*. "We need to tell Heart what is going on. She'll be scared to death if she sees an ambulance coming up the drive. And she'll want to go to the hospital." She would need to prepare for that.

"I agree." He rubbed a hand over his face. "I'd completely forgotten about her." Shifting the phone to his other ear, he added, "I think you need to go talk to her."

"You sure?"

"Positive. She doesn't know me from Adam."

"I hate to leave Levi." He knew that he wasn't doing anything but maybe providing some comfort, but it felt wrong to leave him completely alone.

"I'll stay by his side," Alan replied. Looking determined, he added, "I'm on the phone with the dispatcher. If his condition changes, I'll need to tell her, anyway. It makes sense for me to stay here."

Knowing Alan was right, Clayton got to his feet. "Okay. I'll go speak to Heart." Looking down at Levi's horribly damaged arm and the blood on his clothes, Clayton felt even more at a loss. Levi's condition looked worse with every passing minute. "I'll hurry."

Alan's brown eyes darkened. "I know you're concerned about Levi, but there's nothing either of us can do besides wait and pray. The ambulance is on its way, but until it arrives, everything is in God's hands. Go and talk to her. Give her a moment to process it, okay? I promise, you've got a minute or two, and I don't think it's going to do that girl any good to stand in here and helplessly watch her father."

"You're right." Realizing that he not only had to trust in God, but also this man he barely knew, Clayton strode toward the house.

When he exited the barn, he was shocked to see that snow had started to fall again. The weather had changed without his even realizing it.

Maybe it was the reminder he'd needed. Slowing his steps, he looked up at the sky. "*Danke, Got.* You are right. Our fate is in your hands. Please give me the strength to do your will."

Not exactly feeling better, but assured that he was doing the right thing, he entered the house to find Heart. He just hoped he could find the right words to tell her the news.

Chapter 27

Even though over an hour had passed since both her father and Clayton skipped the meal that she'd worked all morning to prepare, Heart was still mad.

That was the perfect description, too. She wasn't hurt, annoyed, or even irritated. She was mad.

That straight, unvarnished emotion felt good, too. Almost cleansing.

For so long, she'd swallowed her pride whenever her father failed to notice that the floors were sparkling clean, a pie she made had turned out particularly well, or that she'd canned several quarts of chicken stock.

She'd told herself that such things didn't matter, especially because what she did wasn't as important as her father's work. She'd almost begun to believe the same thing. Cooking and cleaning—no matter how well done—didn't make one's life that much better. It certainly didn't bring in any money. Especially not when compared to the sculptures her father created. People paid lots and lots of money for them.

And even though her father had no interest in fame, she'd seen articles written about his work. The authors used words like "inspired," "beautiful," and "transcendent." She'd had to look that word up to try to figure out how a piece of metal could be described as such.

Therefore, making a perfectly roasted chicken with mashed potatoes, fresh beans, and homemade rolls paled in comparison. At least that was what she'd told herself. But then Clayton's arrival and his obvious appreciation for everything she did changed her mind.

She'd started to believe that maybe her efforts weren't so inconsequential after all. That maybe she mattered, too.

And maybe getting to know Mary had helped her, too. Mary had reminded her again and again that every person on God's earth was special, and that even doing something as simple as providing a comforting environment for a rat had value.

As she ran a cloth along already-spotless counters, Heart realized she needed to calm down. *The Lord might understand that you're mad, but that doesn't mean any good is going to come of it. Look at things another way. Now you don't have to prepare another meal for supper tonight. Relax.*

Yes, that was what she needed to do.

Tossing the cloth on the counter, Heart walked into the living room. She had a new book from the library, and she had a needlepoint project that her mother had given her long ago.

Hearing a squeak, she smiled. "And I have you to entertain, don't I, Spike?"

The rat, who'd been playing with some plastic balls that Mary had dropped off for him, gazed at her expectantly.

"You're right, Spike. There's no reason to make you stay in your cage. Just do me a favor and don't run and hide, okay?"

Spike twitched his nose.

She took that as a positive sign. Opening up the cage door, she held out a hand and was pleased when the rat crawled right out to greet her.

Cradling him in her hands, she marveled again that such a small animal could be blessed with such a big personality. "Maybe I need to read up on activities for you. I have a feeling that a bored rat could be a dangerous thing. What do you think? I bet the librarian could help me find a book about fancy rats."

Instead of looking interested, Spike curled into a ball. She knew by now that was his way of cuddling. Her insides melted as she carried him to her father's favorite chair and sat down. Tucking her feet under the fabric of her skirt, she took a cleansing breath and placed the rat on her lap. Spike moved around a bit and looked up at her.

She could swear that he was looking right into her

eyes. "I'm better, Spike. I was in a bit of a dither, but I've calmed down. Thank goodness."

Spike, seeming to understand every word, journeyed to the crook in her arm and snuggled closer. His little warm body made her heart beat a tiny bit faster. She'd always wanted to be a pet-sitter. Maybe it was time to finally do something about that goal.

Yes, she could talk to her father and make plans. Of course, he'd be annoyed that she might not be around to wait on him hand and foot, but he'd understand. If anyone saw the value of putting one's job first, it was he.

Maybe she would only pet-sit a few days a week? That would be a good way to start out. She could make some flyers and hand them out. Maybe even ask Mary to spread the word. Or some of her father's customers who lived nearby.

She'd just started mentally designing her flyer when she heard the door open. Spike raised his head. When she heard the telltale stomp of dirty boots on the kitchen floor, she muttered, "Looks like Daed has decided to finally get something to eat." Feeling a bit peevish, she whispered, "I am not going to run to the kitchen to greet him. I'm not. Not just yet."

"Heart? Heart, where are you?"

It was Clayton. Irritated by the thought that he was now messing up the clean floor, she didn't even bother standing up. "I'm in here. Don't you come in with your dirty boots, though."

To her dismay, he ignored her!

He stomped through the kitchen and into the room. "Heart, I need to tell you something."

Oh, she would just bet he did. Well, she had something to tell him, too, starting with the fact that she didn't appreciate his ignoring her wishes!

Fuming now, she deposited Spike on the chair and got to her feet to face Clayton. "You may think that I don't have anything better—"

Suddenly Heart took notice of his face. It was pale and his eyes looked ravaged. And his clothes . . . were stained with blood. "What's happened?"

Clayton's perfect jaw clenched before he reached out for her hand. "Heart, I'm so sorry to tell you this, but there's been an accident."

She rushed toward him. Taking his hand in both of hers, she squeezed. "It looks like you did have a bit of one. Did you cut yourself? When—"

"Heart, it's your father."

It took a second for his statement to register. "Daed?"

As he gazed at her intently, a muscle jumped in his jaw. It was obvious that he was attempting to find the right way to tell her the news.

She couldn't take the suspense. "What happened?"

"Heart, I'm so sorry, but he's in a bad way. An ambulance should be here any minute."

He needs an ambulance? "Nee." Heart dropped his hand as she shook her head. Every part of her was refusing to hear what he was saying. It simply didn't make sense. "Clayton, *mei daed* doesn't have accidents. He's very strong."

His caramel-colored eyes softened. "*Jah*, he is very

strong, but he is still human. Accidents happen, ain't so?" He took another breath. "It was a bad accident. I think his arm is broken."

The tension in her body eased. All right, then. An accident was bad, and a broken arm was a shame, but it wasn't life-threatening. He'd have a cast and be grumpy, but he'd be fine. She nodded until the fact that there was blood all over Clayton's clothes registered. A broken arm didn't bleed like that. "Where did the blood come from?"

He reached for her again, this time running a hand around her shoulders. Carefully pulling her closer.

Feeling as if she was in a terrible dream, she allowed it. "He's been burned as well. Badly. He's going to need to go to the hospital and likely have surgery." He stared at her. "Do you understand?"

Accident. Ambulance. Hospital. Surgery. Blood. Lots of blood.

One by one, her brain was cataloging the words, shuffling them around, forcing her to make sense of each. And then, to her dismay, tears filled her eyes.

"*Ach*, Heart. I'm so sorry." When she reached for him, intending to circle her hands around his neck, he pulled back. "Darling, don't. You're going to get dirty. I don't want to get blood on you."

"I don't care." She was surprised that he'd called her "darling." Or that the sweet word soothed her. She wasn't sure what to think about that. Not yet.

"All right, then." He pulled off his shirt, leaving him in just the undershirt he liked to wear. The tight-fitting garment showed off all his muscles, leaving no doubt that he was strong, too. Strong enough to do hard jobs. Strong enough to tell her hard news—and to comfort her, too.

And just like that, he bent down slightly and pulled her against him. He was warm and solid. He wrapped his hands around her waist, while Heart curved her arms around his neck. They were hugging. No, they were locked in an embrace. Clayton smelled good and was whispering sweet, soothing words in her ear.

He felt like everything she'd ever needed.

She burst into tears. And then, while she cried into his chest, she could've sworn he kissed her hairline, just at the edge of her *kapp*.

"I know, Heart," he whispered. "Darling girl, I know. You cry all you want." He began rubbing the middle of her back. Softly. As if he was afraid a firmer touch might bruise her.

She needed to get herself together. Her father was hurt and an ambulance was on the way. Her brain knew that, but still she was trembling.

"Shh. Hush now. It'll be okay. You're not alone, Heart. You are not alone."

"I . . . I . . . thank you." Heart took a deep breath. A mixture of laundry detergent and Clayton met her senses. He smelled so good and clean and fresh.

She realized then that he was breathing deep, too.

When he exhaled, a shudder ran through him. It told her that he was hurting, too. He needed her as much as she needed him. Running a hand along her back, he whispered, "Heart. I know you're upset, but we need to head to the barn."

As if on cue, the sound of a shrill, high-pitched siren cut through the air. The ambulance.

Pulling out of his embrace, she said, "I need to get my purse . . . and do you think Daed needs anything?" Should she bring him a fresh shirt?

"Nee." Looking down at himself, he frowned. "I'm gonna run to my room and get a fresh shirt. You get your cloak and put on your boots."

"All right." As she moved into the mudroom, she tried to figure out which shoes to wear.

"Hey, Heart?" Clayton said when he reappeared.

She turned. "Yes?"

"Here is your missing best boot," he said, reaching into the back of the nearby bureau.

She gaped at him. "What? How did you get it?"

"It's a long story, but suffice it to say that a puppy did some damage and I did the rest."

Running a hand along the top of the boot, she saw dozens of tiny tears and chews. Noticed the lace was also broken. But it was her favorite boot, the one that fit her perfectly.

After she'd debated for a second, she slipped it on her foot and then put the other on as well. On another day she'd ask Clayton about why it had disappeared. At the moment, however, she simply didn't care.

"We need to go, Heart."

"I know."

She allowed him to help her put on her cloak, and

then followed him out the door. Only later would she remember that she'd left Spike lounging on her father's chair. She hoped he wouldn't chew a hole into the upholstery and make a nest.

But try as she might, Heart couldn't seem to care if that happened. Not one bit.

Chapter 28

Heart was trembling. Though the snow was falling and the temperature had dropped, Clayton knew her shudders had nothing to do with the weather. If anything, she was probably oblivious to the temperature. She was likely in shock.

Every tender emotion that he'd tried so hard to keep hidden surfaced as his protective instincts kicked in. Even though she wasn't his to protect, Clayton told himself that he was the only person available. Besides, he wanted no one else to be caring for her or looking out for her needs. Yeah, he'd slipped and had called Heart "darling" and "darling girl" out loud. As far as he was concerned, Heart Beachy actually *was* his darling.

Keeping close to her side, he said, "I know you're scared, but I'm right here."

She stared up at him with those blue eyes that never ceased to amaze him. "Promise?"

And there went his insides. Turning to mush. "I promise."

They exited the house just as an ambulance pulled up to the barn. At least the crew had known to turn off the sirens so the horses wouldn't be frightened.

Heart's footsteps slowed as three people climbed out of the flashing vehicle.

"Hey," one of the men said. "Are you Alan? We received a call about a Levi Beachy. We couldn't find an address on the street. Are we at the right place?"

Seeing that Heart was in no condition to answer, Clayton strode forward. "I'm not Alan—he's inside the barn with Levi. But, yes, you're in the right place. My name is Clayton Glick, and this is Levi's daughter, Heart Beachy."

As two of the men strode through the door that Alan had just opened, the third walked to them. "Heart, you say?"

Heart started to nod, then seemed to collect herself. "Yes."

"Okay. Heart, my name is Graham." Speaking softly and slowly, he continued. "We're going to check your father out and then—"

"Hey, Graham! We need the stretcher!"

Graham tensed. "On it!" he called back. "Excuse

me, miss," he said as he turned back toward the ambulance.

Clayton stepped forward. "Do you need a hand?"

"I got it."

Heart's eyes widened as they watched Graham open the back of the ambulance, pull out a metal contraption that was obviously a stretcher on wheels, and push it to the barn. Seconds later, Graham was out of sight.

"Clayton, I need to see him."

He ached to protect Heart. She'd been through enough with her mother dying. He knew how much blood was on the floor of the workshop. He knew how bad Levi's wound looked. He wanted to shield her from seeing something that she would never be able to *un*see, but Clayton knew that wasn't possible. Heart wasn't a little girl and deserved to see her father—no matter what his condition. Besides, he might feel as if she was his, but she wasn't. He wasn't actually anyone but her father's apprentice.

"All right. Come on, then."

He walked her through the door that Alan was holding open. Clayton had a split second to exchange a look with the other man before focusing his attention on Heart again.

When she let out a small moan, he pressed a hand to the small of her back. Levi was now lying on his back on the ground. One of the paramedics was starting an IV line in the uninjured hand. The other man was looking into Levi's eyes with a small light.

Clayton blew out a breath of air he hadn't even realized he'd been holding. "Your father's awake." Hopefully, she didn't hear his relief.

"I need to go to him."

"No, we need to stay here," he corrected. When she ignored his words and stepped forward, Clayton wrapped a hand around Heart's waist to prevent her from going any closer. Lowering his head, he whispered in her ear, "We need to stay out of the way, Heart. These men know what they're doing. Let them do their jobs."

"But—"

There was so much pain in that one word. Leaning down again, he whispered, "Darling, I know. But you need to be strong for him, *jah?*"

"*Jah.* But he's my *daed.*"

Somehow, even though Levi was surrounded by two paramedics, and was in obvious pain, he turned his head toward her voice. "Heart? Heart, are ya here?"

"*Jah.* I'm here, Daed," she said as Graham and the other paramedics secured Levi to the stretcher and checked and double-checked all the monitors they'd attached to him.

"Child." He seemed to struggle. "Are you alone? Clayton?"

"I've got her, Levi," Clayton called out as he guided her to the back of the workshop so the paramedics could maneuver the stretcher out of the room.

"But—"

"Levi, your daughter's okay," the man closest to him said in a calm, firm tone as he stood up. "She's being taken care of. We need you to concentrate on yourself for a moment, okay?" He didn't wait for a response as the three men continued to carefully wheel out the stretcher.

Though it was obvious Levi was trying very hard to be silent, a cry burst from his lips. Next to her *daed*, Heart flinched. If they were alone, or if he'd been her beau or her husband, Clayton would've pulled her into his arms. He wouldn't have cared who was there or whether or not it was appropriate.

But he wasn't that man. She wasn't his. Not yet, anyway. All he could do was stand beside her and give her as much support as she would allow.

Heart, Alan, and he remained silent as one of the men spoke into a radio, while the others spouted off numbers and spoke quietly to Levi.

Levi's eyes were now closed.

After the two other techs navigated the stretcher out of the building, Graham stayed behind to talk.

"What's going to happen?" Heart asked.

"We're taking him to the hospital in Wooster, miss."

"Can I ride with you? Please?"

"I'm sorry, ma'am, but there's not enough room." Clayton knew there really wasn't enough space, but it was also obvious that the paramedics were really worried about Levi's condition—and maybe even concerned about his chances of survival. The last thing they wanted was his daughter in the way in case things got worse.

Her eyes widened. "But—"

As if he was suddenly noticing her *kapp*, Graham said, "Listen, I'll call the dispatcher. She'll find a deputy or someone to come out here and pick you up."

"Okay." Her voice was small. Defeated.

"I'll take you," Alan said. "Don't worry about a thing. I'll take both of you."

He'd completely forgotten about Alan. "Thank you," Clayton said.

"Think nothing of it," Alan said as he followed Graham outside.

"You take care, miss," the paramedic said as he climbed into the driver's side of the vehicle.

They watched one of the other men join the third crew member and Levi in the back. Seconds later, they drove down the driveway.

When they reached the main road, the driver turned the ambulance's lights and sirens on and sped off. Soon they were out of sight.

Clayton glanced at Heart. Tears were in her eyes again, but she was holding her chin and jaw stiff and firm. It was as if she was willing herself not to cry.

He hated that. He didn't want her thinking that she had to put on a show for him or Alan. He wanted her to trust that he would respect all her emotions.

"Alan, let me help you load your horse."

"If it's all the same to you, I'd rather we put him in a stall, and I'll unhitch the trailer. After I drop you kids off at the hospital, I'll come back around and load Buck myself."

"Are you sure?"

"Yeah." Looking at Heart, he said, "I'd rather make sure you two get to the hospital quickly. Maybe I'll even stop by the ranch and get one of the hands to come over. We'll water your horse and clean up a bit. You know, make sure everything is in good order."

Clayton knew Alan was referring to the workroom and the blood and debris on the floor. "Thank you."

"I already put the fire out, son, but you can go check it while I get my truck."

"Thank you, I will." He glanced at Heart. She hadn't moved. He didn't want to leave her alone, but he also didn't want her to see the blood on the floor. "I'll be right back. Stay here, okay?"

"Okay."

"Heart, you come with me," Alan said. "I need to turn on the truck, anyway. You can sit in the cab while I see to Buck and get the trailer unhitched."

Her eyes darted to his. It was obvious that she was in such a fog, she wasn't sure what to do.

Clayton nodded. "I think that's a real good idea." Lowering his voice, he added, "I know you're anxious to get to the hospital, but they're likely not going to let us see your *daed* right away."

"This won't take long," Alan said.

"All right."

Heart looked frailer than Clayton had ever seen her, and he watched as she walked to Alan's side and accepted his help climbing into his big truck.

As Clayton turned to the workshop, he said another prayer, asking the Lord to look out for her. She was going to need His support right now.

Two hours later, Clayton felt as out of place as if he was in the middle of a college campus. Alan had dropped them off at the entrance to the emergency room. The kind man had even volunteered to park his truck and help them talk to the receptionist, but Clayton had refused. Alan had already done enough.

He hadn't expected that they'd be received so coolly in the hospital.

The man at the reception desk had taken their names and information and told them to sit down and wait. When Clayton told him that Heart needed to know how her father was, he'd said that he would tell her about her father when there was news.

Clayton had been frustrated, especially since Heart had looked crushed. When an hour passed, and there still was no news, he'd walked to the man again. This time the male employee had been joined by a woman. When the man rudely cut Clayton off, the woman shook her head.

"I'm sorry you haven't heard anything. We're short-staffed up here. I'll go find out what's going on."

True to her word, she'd found Clayton and Heart just a few minutes later. Leading them to a small, far quieter sitting area, she sat down across from them at the table.

"Your name is Heart, miss?"

"It's Hazel, but everyone calls me Heart."

"I like Heart. My name is Jill." After glancing at Clayton, who gestured for her to go ahead and tell them the news, Jill said, "Heart, your father is in surgery. He had a compound fracture in his arm. He also had received a sizeable wound and burn. So, ah, a burn specialist is being brought in from Cleveland."

"Is he going to be okay?"

"I believe so," Jill said quietly. "The nurse I spoke to is a good one. She told me that your father's life isn't in danger. But he's going to be in surgery for quite a while. They need to repair the bones and the tissue that was damaged. Then they're going to keep him sedated until the doctor from the burn unit arrives. You likely won't be able to see him tonight."

"Are you sure? Everything is going to take that long?"

"Very sure. Plus, he wouldn't know you were in the room, anyway. He's going to be on a lot of painkillers."

She bit her lip. "I . . . That's too bad."

The nurse sent her a sympathetic smile. "I know it's hard. Sometimes I think these moments are harder on family members than on the patients. Do you two have any place you can go to sleep?" She crossed her legs. "Maybe even a motel nearby? I can make sure someone calls you the moment your father comes out of surgery."

"I don't want to leave," Heart said.

Jill's expression turned even more compassionate.

"I know you're worried and upset. But take it from me, sitting in this waiting room isn't going to make the waiting any easier."

"I understand, but I still want to stay." After a pause she added, "My *mamm* has already gone to Heaven. He is all I have left."

"I understand." Jill's gaze flickered to Clayton's again before she stood up. "Here's my card. It has a phone number that will get you directly to someone on staff who can tell you about your father's progress. If you change your mind and leave, this information will be helpful."

"Thank you, Jill," he said. "That is kind of you."

When she was almost at the door, she said, "There's also a cafeteria in the main building. I can give you some vouchers if you'd like. They'll pay for your meal."

Clayton replied again. "Thank you. May we stay here?"

"Yep. Stay in this room as long as you like." She paused, then added, "Heart, I know it's hard, but keep thinking positive thoughts and praying. I've seen a lot of miracles happen here."

"I will," Heart said.

As Jill returned to the reception area, Clayton turned to Heart. "What would you like to do? I can hire a driver to take us back to the farm and give Jill your father's work phone number. I'll sleep next to the phone in his office so there won't be any chance of our missing any news."

"I don't want to leave, Clayton." Staring up at him with blue eyes that appeared luminescent, she said, "Please don't make me go."

He knew right then that he was putty in her hands. His entire being wanted to see to her needs and make her happy. Which made his next words about the easiest he'd ever spoken. "I'm not going to make you do anything. Not tonight."

"Thank you."

Her sweet, grateful smile reached deep inside him. He knew then that he loved her. He loved her, and somehow, someday, she would be his to take care of.

Reaching out, he cradled her hand between his. "Of course, Heart."

Chapter 29

"Daed!"

Heart opened her eyes with a start. She was breathing hard, as if she'd been running as fast as her legs could carry her. She tried to catch her breath.

Little by little, she realized where she was. Not in Wooster. Not in the hospital. She was back in Apple Creek. Back on her farm and snug in her own bed.

Her brain still foggy, she stretched her legs and realized she had put on her nightgown. When they'd first arrived, she'd checked on the puppies and Virginia, who had been looked after by friends of Alan's, and then she'd tended to Spike. Afterward, she'd fallen asleep on top of her quilt, fully dressed. Hours later, she'd summoned enough energy to take a hot shower, split a can of soup with Clayton, and then crawled under her covers.

So . . . another set of hours had passed. The room was dark, and not just because of the thick shades on her windows. Morning hadn't come yet.

She'd been dreaming.

With some dismay she realized that her cheeks were damp. She'd been crying in her sleep. Crying as she'd watched her father bleed onto the kitchen floor.

"It was just a dream," she told herself aloud, in a firm tone. "Daed is safe. He's recovering in the hospital and you are back home. And he never bled on the kitchen floor. That is simply your imagination going bonkers."

She sat up, wiped her face with a tissue, and then looked at the digital clock on her bedside. It was five in the morning. Too early to get up, but too late to spend the next twenty to thirty minutes attempting to fall back asleep. She was up for the day.

"Okay, then," she muttered.

She'd just slipped on her robe, when Clayton knocked on her door. "Heart? Are you all right?"

He had heard her yell. She'd woken him up. "I'm okay!" she replied at last. "I'm sorry I woke you." She listened for his footsteps walking away, but there was only silence.

"You didn't wake me," he said, obviously standing right on the other side of the door.

"Are you sure?"

"Very sure." After a small pause he asked, "Do you need anything?"

"*Nee.* I only had a bad dream. I'm better now."

After another few seconds passed, he spoke again. "Would you like me to bring you a cup of coffee? It would be no trouble."

"You made coffee?"

His chuckle floated through the door, lightening her mood and lifting her spirits. "I did, Heart. So, coffee with milk and sugar?"

"Yes, please," she replied before considering whether it was proper or not.

"Good. I'll be right back."

She leaned against the pillows and exhaled. The chance to sip hot coffee, which she hadn't prepared, as she sat up in bed felt like the height of luxury to Heart. Or maybe it was more like being very spoiled. She had no idea.

All she knew was that it sounded wonderful, like the best thing that had happened to her in forty-eight hours. With some dismay she reckoned it probably was.

It had been a very difficult two days. She and Clayton had waited in that little private room in the hospital for five hours before receiving word that her father was out of surgery and in recovery. During that time she'd cried, worried herself sick, and wrapped herself in so much guilt and regret that it was a wonder she'd been able to stand up.

After receiving word that her father had pulled through, but still wasn't allowed to receive visitors, and wouldn't for some time, Clayton had encouraged her to return home.

He'd left her side, going to arrange a ride home for them. He'd returned to their private space minutes later, a shocked expression on his face.

Fearing that he'd just received even more terrible news, she gasped, "What happened?"

Instead of walking to her side, Clayton had held out a hand for her to take. "Come see. It's something good. I promise."

She'd clutched his hand like the lifeline it was . . . and then had gaped at the sight in the main waiting room. Three Amish families, Mary Miller, and four or five *English* ones were all there.

She and Clayton soon learned that everyone in the vicinity had heard about the ambulance leaving their farm. Alan, who'd called in friends to help load his horse, clean up the workroom, and look after the animals, had filled folks in.

Later, he'd instituted a phone tree to spread the word about Levi's injuries. The preacher and bishop asked everyone to pray. Everyone had stopped everything they were doing to pray for Levi and Heart, and asked how they could help—either financially or by pitching in at the farm.

It was wondrous.

While Heart had gaped at the crowd, Clayton relayed the news about her father making it to the recovery room, but not being able to receive visitors.

Turning to Heart, he added, "I came out here to see if someone at the reception desk could help us get a ride home and something to eat . . . and learned that we had both rides and food to spare."

Even though she'd thought she was out of tears, Heart's eyes filled again. "Thank you all so much."

Mary stepped forward. "We're your friends, child. We care for you and for Levi." Smiling at Clayton, she added, "And you as well, Clayton. You're part of our community now. Whatever you two need, we want to help."

Next thing she'd known, people were organizing transportation. One family volunteered to take her and Clayton back to the house, as well as Mary. It seemed a couple of people wanted to make sure that no rumors were going to start about Heart and Clayton being alone in the house without a chaperone.

Returning to the present, she wondered if Mary was awake now as well.

After quickly donning a pair of warm tights and a favorite old dress that was particularly warm, she brushed her hair and fastened it in a low bun on the base of her neck.

Just as she'd slipped on her *kapp*, Clayton knocked at the door again.

Now feeling a bit foolish, she opened it.

"You're dressed."

"I felt silly lazing about in a nightgown while you were fetching me coffee."

"May I come in?"

"Of course." She backed up to allow him space, then

smiled, because he didn't just have a simple mug in his hands. He was holding a tray with a small carafe and a plate of scones. "What is all this? No, where did it come from?"

He smiled. "Concerned friends and neighbors. Two baskets were on the front porch when I went to feed the horses and gather eggs."

"You did that, too?"

"I did." His eyes warmed. "Where should I put this tray down? It's getting heavy."

"Oh! Gosh, how about on the table by the chair?"

"That looks good to me." After setting it down, he gestured to the chair. "Come sit down and have your snack."

"I'm embarrassed you went to so much trouble. Or did Mary do this?"

"Mary? *Nee.* I haven't seen her yet." He gestured for her to drink.

Heart took a tentative sip and decided that it was the best cup of coffee she'd ever had in her life. Being able to enjoy both a drink and a snack that she hadn't made with her own two hands felt like a precious gift. "The coffee's good, Clayton."

"I'm glad you think so."

"I'm, ah, glad that Mary is still asleep. I mean, I was worried I might have woken her up."

"I doubt that was possible. She not only has Virginia and all the puppies with her, but your cry wasn't that loud. I just happened to be listening for you."

His explanation didn't exactly ring true, but she

wasn't sure why she felt that way. "What are you doing now? I mean, beyond bringing me scones and coffee."

"Not much to do at the moment, now that the morning chores are done."

"Then, would you mind sitting in here with me while I eat?" When he hesitated, she added, "Please?"

After looking to make sure her bedroom door was still open, he nodded. "Sure," he said. "I'm happy to do whatever you need me to do."

Her insides did a little happy dance as he sat down on the ottoman next to her chair.

Clayton might not realize it, but he'd just made what promised to be a difficult day a whole lot better.

Chapter 30

Clayton was exhausted. During the three long days since Levi's accident, he'd been juggling so many emotions, it was a wonder his body knew whether to laugh or cry.

Or, perhaps, he'd do both at the same time.

Standing in the barn after tending to Becket's supper, he found himself leaning against the horse's flank for support. The gelding didn't budge, but it was obvious he didn't know what to do with Clayton.

"Sorry, horse," he said as he walked out of the stall and headed back to the house. "You've got to get it together, man," he muttered to himself.

For at least the hundredth time.

It was snowing again. Nothing too major, just enough

to decorate the ground and remind everyone that Christmas was just around the corner.

Clayton hoped and prayed that they'd be able to celebrate many blessings that Christmas. Or, at the very least, that Levi would be back home and feeling better.

The poor man was still in the hospital, and likely to be there another two days at least. The doctors had put several screws in his broken arm and had to do a skin graft for his burned skin. They'd taken some skin from his side, so now he had a broken arm, a wound on his arm, and another on his side.

Since infection was a danger, Levi was essentially quarantined. It was an understatement to say he wasn't handling the isolation, pain, and forced inactivity well.

When they'd visited that morning, Levi had been so gruff, Mary had encouraged Heart and him to leave. There was no way to help Levi besides ignoring his complaints and counseling patience. Neither he nor Heart was the best person to sit at his bedside.

Heart worried for her father and therefore took all his complaints to heart. Clayton, because of his feelings for Heart, found himself concentrating more on her than Levi.

When they got back to the farm, Clayton knew it was just as well they'd left. Horses still needed shoes, and clients still wanted to pick up their finished pieces of art. Levi had given him the okay to do what he could in the shop.

It was a change for them, but not a completely awkward one. With each week on the Beachy farm, Clayton had done more and more work. Even better, a lot of Levi's longtime customers were beginning to trust him. One had even gone so far as to say that he didn't know what Levi had done without Clayton. That had made him feel good. He wanted to help Levi, not be another cause of worry.

Continuing to stand in the snow, Clayton wondered how he and Heart should spend the rest of the evening. He'd already cleaned, fed, and watered Becket, and had even taken him outside to the corral for a bit.

Jerry had passed away two days ago, so now Mary was dividing her time between visiting Levi in the hospital and staying at the house with them. He'd told her when they were at the hospital that morning to take her time returning to the farm.

He knew that Heart was in good hands, and Mary knew that her role of chaperone was unnecessary. Clayton might be falling in love with Heart, but the only thing he wanted to do was care for her and the farm.

That meant it was going to be a very quiet evening with too much time for Heart to worry. He needed something to take her mind off Levi and keep her busy.

Only then did he remember the mess in the basement. Someone needed to go down there, clean it up, and put all the boxes in some semblance of order. It might as well be him.

Pleased to have thought of something useful to do, he went back into the house.

Heart was sitting listlessly at the table. "Do you

need something, Clayton? The Weavers brought over supper. I haven't heated it up yet."

"Let's wait a bit to eat. I'm not too hungry."

"I'm not hungry, either," she said. "Are you going to take a rest now?"

"Actually, I was thinking of something better for us to do."

"Oh? What?"

"I thought you might like to order me around the basement for a spell."

She sat up a little bit straighter. "What do you have in mind?"

Her expression had perked up. He hid a smile. Obviously, the thought of bossing him around had some appeal. That was adorable.

He folded his hands across his chest and attempted to look nonchalant. "So . . . I was thinking about all those boxes and how out of order everything was."

"It is a mess down there."

"I think it's a fine project for me to work on. Now, I don't mind organizing it for you, of course, but I'm going to need your help. You're going to tell me what you want done."

There was a spark in her eyes. Almost for the first time since the accident. "That's so kind of you . . . but I couldn't allow you to do that."

"Of course, you can."

"Clayton, you were hired as an apprentice. This feels like we're taking advantage of you."

"I don't feel that way. Come now. Don't you think we've already blurred the lines? I mean, we've looked for rats, carted around puppies, and sat vigil in a hospital waiting room."

"You are wonderful and have gone above and beyond, time and again. But—"

"But *nothing*. Come on, then. We need more than one flashlight, too. We can position them down so we can see everything. Where are your extras?"

"In here." She picked up two. "This will give us three lights down there."

"That'll do." He led the way downstairs. When they reached the pile of boxes, he had the same thought he'd had the first time he'd spied them. The disorganized mess was out of character for the Beachy farm.

Now he rather thought the pile was a symbol of how things were for Heart and Levi, and maybe even himself, too. Everything was ninety percent together, but there was still some disarray that needed to be tended to.

Perhaps that was how it was for everyone; there was always something out of sight that was so hard to deal with, it was tempting to push it aside and hope it would be forgotten. He'd surely done that with his feelings about being given up for adoption.

Even if this pile of boxes was nothing more than a symbol of how busy Heart and Levi were, Clayton hoped he could do something to help them get everything put back to rights.

Standing in front of it all, he wondered if the easiest thing for Heart would be to simply get rid of some boxes. "Is there anything you want to throw out?"

"I don't think so." Looking a bit embarrassed, she said, "That's part of the problem down here. So many of these things were my mother's. Or they are memories from my grandparents or great-grandparents. I'm not sure what Daed wants to keep and what he doesn't care about."

"What about you? What do you want to keep?"

"Not much of it. I firmly believe in the Amish way of honoring our ancestors. We cherish and honor memories, not things. Since I didn't really know my grandparents or great-grandparents, some of the items in these boxes don't mean much to me."

"What does your father do with his family's things?"

"Daed? Oh, he doesn't have anything from his family."

"Oh?"

"I'm sorry, for some reason I thought you knew his background. You see, *mei dad* lost his parents young and then went to work when he was fourteen."

"So he's an orphan, too."

"*Jah.* In a way." Her voice lowered to a whisper. "I think he might understand your pain about living in the children's home better than you realize."

"I should talk to him about it. Or is it a sore subject?"

"I don't think it is. Daed always said that God

watched over him instead of his parents. He is very faithful."

"I noticed that." Appreciating their conversation, especially since it was helping Heart think about something besides her father's accident, Clayton added gently, "It's a good quality to have, don't you think?"

Her expression softening, Heart nodded. *"Jah."*

As he shared that smile, everything inside of him yearned to lift her spirits. But he wasn't her man. He wasn't anything to her right now. He was just a man trying to make something of himself. He knew that he wanted to protect her from pain and shield her from further hurts. But he certainly didn't have that right.

So instead of giving her a hug or promising his help, he focused on the mess in front of them. He could help her with that.

"Where do you think we should begin?"

She put her hands on her hips as she looked around. "I think we need shelves or something," she said. "Are there extra ones in the barn?"

"I can build you some. Your father has a lot of wood. He uses it for crates when people ask him to ship smaller pieces to them."

"You know how to build shelves?"

"Jah, Heart." At the moment he was so intent on making her happy, he would tell her anything if it meant that the shadows of worry would fade from her expression. "What do you think?"

"I'd hate for Daed to get upset about using the wood for this."

"You live here, too, Heart." He wanted to point out that her father was wealthy enough to buy more wood for crates, or even to buy a set of shelves for his neglected basement if he so desired. But, of course, that wasn't his place.

As she stared at the pile of boxes a little bit longer, Clayton knew she was debating what to do. Just when he was going to offer to simply sweep out the space and restack the boxes, she spoke.

"Okay."

He raised an eyebrow. "Okay to cleaning or okay to building shelves?"

"Okay to building shelves—if you let me help."

"Pardon me?"

Her chin lifted. "Clayton, I want to help you. I want to help build shelves for my mother's things—and to show Daed when he gets home that I helped make everything better."

Clayton wanted to tell her that she already made everything better. Of that, there was no doubt. She made this house a home simply by living there. And then there was everything else she did: the cooking, the cleaning, and her smiles. The way she kept track of everything and everyone—all without expecting any thanks.

One day—if his dreams ever became a reality—he would tell her all of that.

But for now, he only nodded. "I hope you are ready to hammer nails."

"I'm ready. I might not do everything as well as you, but I aim to try."

"Your father told me that one's best is always good enough. I thought that was sound advice."

"Me too." She smiled at him. "Let's get busy."

Chapter 31

Heart had a Christmas wish and it was completely selfish. She wanted Clayton to kiss her by Christmas Day.

She would never admit such a thing to anyone. Honestly, she could barely admit it to herself. She knew she should be ashamed, too. Her father was in the hospital with a terrible burn and a broken arm. He was recovering from surgery and was in a lot of pain. That was what she should be thinking about.

Or she should be giving thanks for Alan and Mary and the doctors and nurses and all of their friends who had done so much for her and her father.

Or, perhaps, she should even be thinking about Spike and her future pet-sitting business. Or something honorable and worthwhile.

But she was so very ready for something to happen for herself. For so long, all she'd ever wanted was to be seen. Not because her mother was sickly and dying. Not because her father was formidable and strong.

Maybe not even for her blue eyes or because the Lord had given her pleasing features.

She wanted to be recognized as Heart. Imperfect, hardworking, romance-reading, a little bit awkward, but essentially kind, Heart.

Unfortunately, almost every man in her circle only ever saw her as an extension of her father. They'd half-heartedly courted her in order to get to know him . . . or even the exact opposite. They'd tried to pull her away from him. They'd made it known that a future with them meant having little to do with Levi Beachy. They didn't understand that she adored her father, but had enough love in her heart for someone else, too.

But Clayton Glick was different. From the moment he'd first seen her, she'd felt his gaze focused entirely on her. The way he'd looked at her made her feel as if no one else existed. The way he listened to her gave her chills.

Nee, it was addictive.

It might not be right, and it might not be something that she should be proud of, but Heart didn't want to give that up—especially since she felt different when she was around him. When she was in Clayton's company, her world seemed to slide into place. As if she'd gone to the chiropractor and suddenly her bones had been adjusted. What she'd used to think was acceptable now seemed misaligned.

She and Clayton fit together. She knew it. And she was selfish enough, or maybe just determined enough, to know that she wanted him in her life.

Heart wanted a memory to treasure. She wanted something special to hold on to. She needed something special to think about in the middle of the night after she'd cooked and cleaned and smiled at everyone and done what she was supposed to do.

She wanted a memory that was perfect and pure and maybe even secret.

"Heart, I think I have it all together!" Clayton called out from his spot next to the back wall of the basement.

"Are you sure?" she teased, just to show him that she wasn't completely impressed with the way he'd surveyed the pile of wood and scraps in the back of her father's workshop and seen the makings of a wall of shelves in the basement.

Together they'd transported all the scraps to the basement, since Clayton pointed out that it might be difficult for the two of them to carry a big, wide set of shelves down the basement stairs.

"Come see," he called out. "Look how well this pile of two-by-fours and the sheets of plywood are going to go together."

"Am I supposed to know what a two-by-four is?"

"Ah . . . yes."

She walked toward him, pretending that her steps were sure. Of course, they weren't. Because while Clayton seemed to be thinking only of wood and shelves and basement cleaning, she was thinking about something a whole lot different.

"Guess what?" he asked.

"What?"

"I have a surprise for you."

"What is it?"

"This! Look what I found for you." He held out both of his hands. One held a hammer. The other held several nails. "Are you ready?"

Was she ready to build bookshelves? No. No, she was not. The truth of the matter was that she'd been willing to say anything to stay near him.

"Sure."

His happy grin dimmed. "You don't sound too excited. Are you nervous about hammering in nails?"

"Not at all." She was only nervous about trying to get him to kiss her.

"I'll help you. Come over here."

Heart walked to where he pointed, which just happened to be by his side. She gripped the hammer and the nail. "I'm ready. Where should it go?"

"I'll hold the pieces together. You hammer in the nail right here," he said. "Ready?"

"Yes." She smiled at him while he lined up the wood. Then, because she had no choice, she neatly hammered in the nail.

"Wait, you already know how to hammer." He frowned. "I didn't expect that."

She couldn't help but giggle. "I know. But, ah, I am my father's daughter. Levi Beachy didn't have a lot of interest in dolls or playing house. And when I was a handful and my mother sent me out to keep him company, he gave me projects so I'd stay away from the forge."

"So he taught you to nail things together."

"*Jah*. And sand and paint. I can do all sorts of things. None of them very well, but I can do them."

"You are full of surprises. I know I'm only here because I wanted to be your father's apprentice, but I'm really glad we met, Heart."

She smiled up at him. "I am, too."

His gaze warmed. She saw his eyes dart to her lips. Felt him lean a little closer. "Here," he said.

She coughed. "Hmm? Oh. Yes. More nails. Thank you." When he pointed to where she should hammer, she pounded a nail into the wood.

"Good job."

"Thanks."

And then they did the same thing again. He pointed; she hammered. Again. And again. He complimented her every so often.

She felt like rolling her eyes. It might be vain, but she had no desire to be complimented for the way she could pound in a nail.

"We're getting a lot done, aren't we?" he asked.

"*Jah.*" They certainly were making progress. Of the, ah, building sort.

The problem was that it wasn't fun.

She appreciated Clayton's patience with her. She reckoned if he wasn't pointing and holding and complimenting her so much, he'd already be done.

She wished he was already done.

After another ten minutes passed, and her arm was beginning to feel a bit sore, she sighed. "I think I need a break."

Clayton looked at the set of shelves, which were only halfway done, and then at her. "Are you sure?"

"Would you mind terribly if I just watched you for a little while?"

"Of course not." Looking as if he was about to slay a predator, he picked up the hammer and efficiently placed a nail. After he smiled at her, he continued. Hammering the pieces together.

Fifteen minutes later, the set of shelves was just about put together.

"I'm almost done. Do you want to hammer in the last nail?"

"Sure." She held out her hand.

"Hey, wait." Clayton placed both hammer and nail on the floor as he searched her face. "You're thinking about something else, aren't you?"

"I'm afraid so."

He stepped closer. "Listen, I know it's hard, but everything will get better. Before you know it, your *daed* will be home."

"I want to kiss you," she blurted. Those five words rang out in the air.

Clayton froze. "Heart?"

Oh, but this is mortifying! Honestly, she didn't deserve to have a boyfriend. No decent, good woman went around telling men that she wanted to kiss them. "Never mind. Let's just forget I said anything." She turned to look for the hammer.

He reached for her shoulders. Turned her to face him. "I've been trying to give you space," he said. "Because you are Heart Beachy and I . . . Well, I am nothing close to that. But you know I like you."

She gazed into his eyes. Saw kindness and patience. Two sweet attributes. Unfortunately, neither of them was making her feel any better. "Maybe I should go upstairs. Check on Spike."

"Spike's fine."

"Or start supper. Would you like meat loaf?"

"*Nee.* I want to kiss you, too."

And then finally, at long last, Clayton was holding her close and brushing his lips against hers. She gripped his biceps when he deepened that kiss. It was sweet. Almost passionate.

When he lifted his head, he stared hard at her. Seemed to search her face. "Heart?" he murmured. "What do you want me to do now?"

It felt like a trick question. Since she had no experience, she wasn't sure what to say. Except for the truth.

"I want you to do what *you* want to do."

Yes, it was a rather garbled mishmash of words. Evasive and not helpful. It was also not the complete truth, because Heart knew exactly what she wanted. She wanted another kiss.

But when Clayton smiled before taking her lips again, she realized that he'd gotten the gist of what she'd meant.

Because this time his one kiss turned into several. Several perfect, intense, terrific kisses. Kisses that surpassed her imagination . . . and she'd imagined a lot. They were everything she'd dreamed of.

When Clayton finally stepped away, his face was flushed and his breath was a little ragged. He ran a hand through his hair. "I, uh, should probably get these shelves done."

"I'll go make us supper. And, um, tend to Spike."

She hurried upstairs before he had time to say another word. As far as she was concerned, that was a good thing. She couldn't think of another word that needed to be said.

Chapter 32

Given Mary's profession, she'd been in a lot of hospital rooms. Since she didn't only help patients at the end of their lives, but also when they were recovering from an illness or surgery, she'd had the opportunity to visit just about every hospital in the area. She liked to think she was a fairly good judge of both the facilities and the staff.

The hospital in Wooster was one of her favorites. The facility served a varied population, given the fact that it was in a college town on the outskirts of both Cleveland and Apple Creek. She knew enough of the staff to appreciate their down-home kindness and their professional credentials.

Levi Beachy was recovering in a good place.

In addition, his hospital room was a fairly good size and looked comfortable enough. It was clean and the walls were painted a soothing gray-blue. The staff was professional and caring. If a person had to be in the hospital, this one was as good a medical place as any.

Unless, it seemed, one was Levi Beachy.

As she looked at the big man, it was obvious that everything about the room was just a little too small. The hospital bed was a tad too short and a bit too narrow for his wide shoulders. The doorway leading into his private bathroom wasn't quite big enough for him to walk inside with his IV cart alongside him.

And, Mary decided, she was beginning to feel that the staff was a little too lenient where he was concerned. Levi Beachy was not a very good patient. If she was his nurse instead of his friend, she would've suggested he behave better.

"I don't think anyone here works very hard," Levi grumbled when she stopped by at around ten o'clock in the morning. "Every time I ask for something, it takes forever."

"Forever's a long time," Mary teased, hoping to pull a smile from his surly frown. And then, perhaps, remind him that the staff had many people to attend to.

His lips didn't even twitch. "I know it. I've been here forever and a day. They should just let me go." Levi shifted, a wince revealing that he was still in a lot of pain. "This bed is going to be the death of me. I can never get comfortable."

Mary felt for him, she really did, but she was starting to feel very, very sorry for the hospital staff.

"The doctor isn't going to release you until you are ready."

He scowled. "I'm ready now." Looking down at his hospital gown, he pulled at it with distaste. "They wouldn't even let me change into some of my regular clothes. I like to wear T-shirts and flannel pajamas to sleep."

"Levi, you know you're not going to be able to wear a T-shirt anytime soon. Your arm is broken."

He frowned at his appendage, as if it had personally offended him. "I haven't forgotten that, Mary."

Her patience was dwindling. "Maybe the doctor will give you some good news today."

"No telling what he'll say . . . or when he'll return." Staring at his door, he continued his mini-tirade. "I haven't seen him since yesterday."

"Levi, you know you aren't being fair."

"Fair?" He rolled his eyes. "Of course, I'm being fair. I'm stuck in this place! All I'm saying is that the man needs to work a full day. All I'm doing is sitting in bed." He waved his right hand. "Where is everyone? I canna even get a nurse to come in."

As if to illustrate his point, a kind-looking nurse started to walk into the room, got a good look at him, and seemed to think better of it. She turned and walked back toward the nurses' station.

"See?" Levi asked.

"You scared her away with your barking and fussing."

"If being here was making me better, I wouldn't be barking or fussing."

"You aren't being fair."

"You're supposed to be on my side, Mary."

Oh, brother. Obviously, it was time for some tough love, and it seemed she was going to be the person to give it. "You know, Levi, I've had some really bad-tempered patients before, but you might take the cake."

He had the gall to look offended. "I think not."

"Levi, I've sat here with you every day since the accident. I know what I'm talking about. You, my friend, are unreasonable and rude. I suggest you consider being a lot kinder very soon."

His eyes widened before narrowing. "Now you're picking on me?"

She'd sat beside him when the doctor and nurses removed his bandages to check on the healing of the graft.

She'd known it had to be painful. But that wasn't the only thing bothering Levi. It was as if focusing on the burned and broken arm brought home the reality of his situation. He was not going to be able to shoe horses or work in his forge or on his art for at least six weeks. Maybe closer to three months.

It might as well have been six years.

The prospect made him grumpy and short-tempered, and he wasn't afraid to let everyone know it.

"I'm not picking on you. Just trying to point out some truths."

He looked ready to argue, noticed the same scared-looking nurse scurry by, and sighed. "Such as what?"

"You actually want to know?"

He gestured with his good arm. "*Jah*. I'm stuck here

listening. I'm your captive audience. So start talking. What did I do that was so wrong this time?"

"This time?"

"*Jah*, Mary. You really should work on your bedside manner. You aren't making me feel very good."

When Levi talked to her like that, she felt both exasperated and curiously amused. The man had a hidden sense of humor that never failed to surprise her. "You know, sometimes I don't know if you're being serious or pulling my leg."

His lips twitched as he treated her to the full force of his blue-eyed stare. "That's a good thing, don't you think?"

Is he flirting?

Feeling he'd just neatly turned the tables on her, she got a little flustered. "I'm not sure. I'm trying to help you get better, you know."

"I know. I'm also grateful that you're giving me so much of your time."

She knew he was being sincere. "Maybe there's nowhere else I'd rather be."

"Maybe?"

His voice was soft and almost smooth. Goodness, but the man was something. Who else but Levi could be as grumpy as a bear, yet still be attractive? "Levi, you know I'm being serious. I'm glad to be here . . . because I'm grateful that you're here. We could've lost you."

"I know. I'm grateful to be here as well."

"You're a healthy, strong man. You'll recover. All of the doctors and nurses have said that."

Some of the humor that had filled his eyes slowly faded. "It's gonna take a while. Maybe a long while."

"I realize that, but you will heal."

"You're right." He shifted again. Sighed. "I hate that I'm letting Heart down. And my customers. I need to get back to work."

"Clayton is doing a good job, and with your neighbor Junior offering to come in every other Tuesday, the majority of the work will get done."

"The farmwork, yes. My artwork, no."

"It's not your right hand that's injured. Maybe someone can help hold things while you weld them together."

"I don't know."

"Levi, I promise, a year from now, this will be a memory."

He blinked. "You said almost the same thing when I broke down a couple of days after Katie died."

Mary felt her cheeks heat. "Did I say that? I don't remember." Of course, she did. Levi had been so strong and stoic during his wife's last days, through the funeral preparations, and all while attempting to console poor Heart. He'd actually been almost too stoic. At times she'd privately compared him to a rock. He'd been solid, but there had been no softness to him.

She'd mistakenly believed that his hard demeanor had meant he lacked something vital—a sympathetic ear or soft emotions for Heart. She'd worried about the girl living the rest of her days without her mother. Feared that Heart would have a rough time living alone with Levi.

Mary had soon realized, of course, that she'd been very wrong.

When she'd found him in the barn, crying silently, his very being so torn up with grief, Mary had begun to cry, too. Not just for the loss of Katie, but for Levi. And maybe for herself. She'd prided herself on being a really good caregiver, who was empathetic and caring. But instead of thinking the best about Levi, she'd made a quick judgment.

Returning to the present, she gazed at him. Noticed that even in a hospital gown, in a hospital bed, he looked as if he could take on the world. If someone he loved was in danger or in pain, he'd sure try.

She swallowed, tasting different words on her tongue, trying different phrases on for size. "Levi, I hope you know that I've regretted the way I was around you at first."

"What do you mean?"

"I should've been more patient. Not expected you to react the way I thought you should." She shook her head. "I'm not explaining myself well. What I mean is that I should've been more giving to you."

"Mary, you were everything Katie needed you to be. That's all that mattered."

"That wasn't enough." Because she knew her job was to help the survivors as much as the dying.

"It was. Because you were also everything that my Heart needed you to be. You gave her a shoulder to cry on and a sweet, kind ear. I've always been grateful for that."

"But I wasn't that way for you."

A line formed between his brows. "I didn't need you to be. I'm a man."

"*Jah*, you are. But you also are human and loved Katie and were mourning."

Levi's eyes watered before he blinked, restoring his usual granite countenance. "Mary, why are we even talking about this? I thought you were here because of my arm." He wiggled the fingers of his left hand. "Don't you want to chastise me some more?"

"Maybe your injury and poor attitude aren't the only reason I'm here."

He froze. "What is the other one?"

He was staring at her. "Maybe I'm here because I care about you."

"I care about you as well." Looking away, he added, "I mean, you're a good caregiver. And a good friend, of course."

"I'm glad you think that." Her bottom lip trembled, but she forced herself to say what had been on the tip of her tongue for so long. "Levi, do you think that there's a chance you'll ever see me as anything other than those things?"

His blue eyes, so perfect and striking, darkened. "If you're asking if I've ever looked at you and felt something more than mere friendship, I have."

"I see." She couldn't help feeling more than a little flat. Yes, he'd answered her question, and maybe even had given her what she'd asked for, too. But was it a declaration that made her insides melt and her pulse race a bit? No.

"Have you felt that way about me?"

His voice was soft. She faced him again and was caught off guard by his expression. It was as tender as an ardent suitor in his first throes of love. And . . . there went her insides. Responding in the way she'd hoped. "Yes."

His lips parted. He tried to move a bit, but due to his gown, all the monitors, and the bed rails, it was obvious he couldn't do much at all. "I canna believe I'm stuck here in this blasted bed."

She chuckled. "You'll be leaving soon."

"That isn't going to help me now, though, is it?" He sighed. "Mary Miller, it looks like you're going to have to do the moving."

"Pardon?"

"Come closer. Put down this stupid rail that I don't need and sit on the side of the bed."

"Why?" And, yes, she felt as if that word had just been choked out of her.

"You know why. So I can reach you."

"Levi, what would someone say if they came in and found us like that?" Of course, the moment she said the words, she realized that she hadn't told him no.

Right away, shouldn't she have told him no?

Triumph gleamed in his eyes. "I don't care. Come on, then."

She was a widow. A caregiver. She was a lot of things. She was Amish and had been raised to be proper and modest.

But, even if she was all those things, it seemed she

wasn't too old to push propriety aside and sit closer to a very attractive man. All because Levi wanted to touch her.

"Mary. Don't make me move myself near you. It'll likely mess up half these monitors and everyone will come running."

She moved. She lowered the rail on the side of his bed, arranged his sheet and blanket a bit so she wouldn't pull it, and then sat down beside him. "Is this better?"

"Jah."

Just as she was going to ask him what exactly he intended to do, he shifted, curved his good hand around her jaw, and then kissed her.

Mary was so startled, she grasped his shoulders.

Or maybe she was simply holding on for dear life because . . . *surprise!* Levi kissed like he worked in his shop. With power and finesse. Like nothing else mattered in the world.

Like he'd been placed on the earth to hold her in his arms and make her entire body feel as if it was on fire.

"Levi, I have your lunch," a new and unfamiliar voice called out.

They broke apart as a volunteer wheeled in a cart. Obviously shocked by what she'd just interrupted, she said, "I'm so sorry."

Mary sat back down on her chair as if she'd just been caught being very, very bad.

"You have my lunch?" Levi asked.

"I do." The volunteer grinned. "You know what? I'm going to put this tray right here," she said as she placed the plastic tray on the small table by the door. "I have a feeling your guest will have no problem taking care of it herself. You are, ah, obviously in good hands."

Mary gaped at the cheeky woman as she turned with a swish of her skirt, then sauntered out and down the hall. "Levi, I have a feeling she's not going to keep what she saw a secret."

But instead of looking upset, he simply looked pleased. "Good. Maybe they'll finally decide to let me out of here."

Chapter 33

Christmas Eve

It wasn't like any Christmas that Heart had ever experienced, but she couldn't say it was a bad day. Actually, with the four of them together and a variety of casseroles, desserts, breads, and side dishes on her mother's sideboard, they were actually eating better than in some years past.

The only thing she regretted was that she didn't have a present for her father, Clayton, or Mary. Because of the accident, her father's lengthy hospital stay, the need to make meals for Clayton, and five puppies intent on causing mischief, she'd had no time.

So it all made sense. Of course, it made sense. And Christmas wasn't about gifts and such, anyway. But she still wished she had presents for everyone.

"Heart, what's got you frowning so?" Daed called out.

She peeked into the living room. He was sitting in his chair in front of the fireplace with a copy of *The Budget* in his right hand. His left arm was encased in a bright blue cast and was resting on one of his chair's arms.

Her father looked as comfortable as it was possible for him to get. He even had a pair of reading glasses perched on his head.

No way did she want to upset him with talk of presents. Or the lack of them. "Nothing."

He set the paper down and rested his eyeglasses on top of it. Then he studied her. "Come over here and talk to me, child."

"I need to get supper ready."

"Even I know that you've got nothing to do besides heat the food."

"There's more to do than that. It's Christmas Eve."

"Ah. It is, ain't so?"

His voice was mild and his eyes were dancing. Heart wasn't sure if he was making fun of her or not. "Daed, this is why I didn't want to talk. You're not going to understand."

"I might if you give me a chance. Heart, please come over here and talk to me. There ain't a thing that's more important than hearing what's on your mind. Now, what's made you sad?"

Not wanting to fight it any longer, she walked into the living room, noticing yet again that the house looked the same as it always did. There was no cinnamon-scented candle burning. No pretty line of Christmas cards decorating the banister. No jar of Christmas cookies. No hidden gift in a closet.

"I just wish it felt like Christmas."

"It doesn't feel like that to you?"

"You know it doesn't."

"What are you missing?"

"Candles and cookies." Everything.

"We have out your mother's red tablecloth."

"I know, but that's all. It just doesn't feel like Christmas Eve. And I know I shouldn't care, Daed. You're out of the hospital and we have each other. I am grateful for that. I really am. I'm being ungrateful and petty."

"Hmm." He looked down at Spike, who seemed to have taken up permanent residence in her father's arms. "The rat seems happy as a clam."

"That's because he has you."

"You have me, too. Ain't so?"

"I know, Daed." She looked away. "Forget I said anything, okay? I know I'm being unreasonable. That's why I didn't want to talk. I must be tired or something."

"Hold on now. I didn't say you were being unreasonable. I mean, I happen to think you have a point."

"You do?"

"What point?" Clayton asked as he and Mary joined them.

"Nothing," Heart said.

"Actually, Heart's upset," her father said. "It seems she's feeling this house looks a bit drab and not befitting of the season."

Mary looked around. "I suppose she does have a point. I don't see a fruitcake in sight."

Heart was slightly offended. "I don't make fruitcakes."

"You don't?" Clayton asked. "That was my favorite dessert at the children's home."

"Really?" And . . . now she felt even worse. "I'm sorry. I should've made you one." If she knew how to make one.

"Oh, Heart." Clayton's voice softened. "You've got to know we're teasing you."

Studying his earnest expression, she felt the same jolt of goodness she always did whenever he was near. "I know. I mean, I guess I knew." She threw up her hands. "I know we're only supposed to be thinking about the birth of Jesus."

"But you wish you were feeling festive, too?"

She smiled at Mary. *"Jah."*

"I'm sorry, Heart," Daed said. "This accident changed everything, didn't it?"

"Don't apologize for almost dying."

"I don't think I was actually near death . . . just injured. In any case, I'm merely stating a fact." He looked at Clayton. "Although I have to admit that I guess I don't feel *un*festive at the moment. I mean, we might have something to celebrate."

"What?" she blurted. Then she felt foolish. After all, it was Christmas Eve.

"I suppose it's up to Clayton," her father murmured. "Pup, what do you think? Is now the time?"

"Here?" He swallowed. "In front of you and Mary?"

"Well, *jah*. I mean, I have a broken arm and I'm holding a rat. You really don't expect me to get up and move, do ya?"

Clayton rubbed a hand over his smooth cheek. "Um, I guess not."

"You could take Heart to another room, I suppose," Mary said. "But, um, I don't know if it would make much difference. Levi and I would probably listen at the door."

Clayton got to his feet. "You're right. I reckon I'll just have to do it here."

"Do what?" Heart asked. Then her breath caught as he stopped right in front of her and took hold of her hands. Both of them. "Clayton?"

"Heart, it's like this. I love you. I've loved you from the first moment I saw you, carrying Spike's cage and looking like a mixture of sunshine and goodness and everything beautiful in this world. The moment I set eyes on you, I knew I'd never find another woman on this earth who was as perfect for me."

"I'm really glad you two didn't leave the room," Mary murmured.

Heart ignored her. "Clayton."

"Breathe, Heart," Daed murmured.

She took a deep breath. "I don't know what to say except that I love you, too."

He smiled. "Truly? I haven't scared you off?"

"My father is Levi Beachy. It takes a lot of gruff to scare me."

"She has a point."

Clayton chuckled. "I don't want to scare you. I want to be everything to you."

"You already are. You've helped me, helped me with the farm, helped my *daed* and Mary and all the clients and even Spike. You've made me happy and made me feel like anything is possible. Even when there's too much work and I'm lonely."

"You're everything I ever dreamed when I was a teenager in that home. I was sure there was goodness and beauty in this world. I'd seen glimpses of it . . . but then I knew that it really did exist when I saw you." Stepping closer, he whispered, "I want to hold on to you, Heart. I want to make sure you're loved every day. I want to make sure you're happy every moment. I want you to be my wife."

Every bit of her stood on end. Wanting to believe what he was saying, but too afraid to trust her ears. "You do?"

"He does," Levi said.

Mary groaned. "Levi, hush."

"Sorry, Mary, but the boy asked for my blessing last night. I'm invested. Besides, I know I'm right."

And then, there Clayton went. On one knee. Right in

front of Mary and Heart's father. In front of Virginia, five puppies, and a rat.

The whole room fell silent.

"Please, Heart, please be my wife. I promise I'll always love you, never track mud on your floor, never make you cry, and never call you Hazel. Heart, will you marry me?"

She'd always imagined that her proposal would be filled with flowers and chocolate and privacy and kisses. But had she ever imagined anyone saying such beautiful words?

Reaching for him, she said the only thing she could. "Yes."

And then he was on his feet, and Mary and her father were laughing, and then Clayton was twirling her around, and all the puppies were barking.

And then, she blinked and they were alone.

"They left. I think they went outside."

"I think your father knew I would never speak to him again if he didn't. I'm so glad you said yes. Thank you, Heart," Clayton said, just before his lips brushed against hers. Then he held her close and held her face in his hands.

And kissed her again, whispering sweet words as he practically feasted on her lips.

Or maybe that was her.

All she knew was that when she opened her eyes again, she was engaged, Clayton was smiling at her, and the entire living room felt bright and happy.

Not too long ago, she'd woken up in the morning

thinking that she needed so many things to turn her life around. To be the woman she and her mother would've been proud of.

She realized now that she'd been so very wrong.

All she'd needed was love.

No, all she'd needed was to remember that she'd been loved—and that she had so much love to give, too.

Epilogue

❧❧❧

Fifteen months later

It was a beautiful spring day, and all the apple trees scattered around town were in full bloom. It also happened to be the perfect day for a wedding.

The event, which had included a bride and groom, two matrons of honor, three preachers, and over four hundred guests, was over. So was the reception under a trio of tents, with an amazing number of rented tables, chairs, kitchen equipment, and at least fifty battery-operated candles. The four hundred or so people who had enjoyed the luncheon had at last gone home.

The fields surrounding the affair would likely never be the same. For most of the day the grounds had been so full of horses and buggies and vehicles and buses that more than one person had said almost every person in the county must have been there. It might not have been an exaggeration.

The crowd had been an eclectic mix, too. Amish and *English*, Ohioans and Canadians. Some folks heard that attendees came from almost every state in the Union. Everyone agreed that it was the biggest wedding the small town of Apple Creek had ever seen, and that was saying a lot, since quite a few nuptials had recently taken place.

By six o'clock that evening the small, relaxed after-party had finished. The only people who remained on the Beachy farm were Heart and Clayton.

And Levi and Mary Beachy, Apple Creek's newest bride and groom. Heart's beloved father and her new stepmother.

One of her father's clients had offered the use of his lake house in Wisconsin for their honeymoon. When her *daed* had taken him up on the offer, another client had stepped in, providing transportation to the house. Not to be outdone, another one of her father's wealthy art clients was providing a way home. Even Mary's son Henry had been generous. He and his wife had supplied the house with food and drinks.

It was going to be quite a honeymoon for her father and stepmother. Heart was so happy for them both.

All she had to do was get them out of the house. The newlyweds' car had arrived almost thirty minutes ago. When the driver pulled up, Clayton had given him a cardboard box filled with a Mason jar of lemonade and two sandwiches, chips, and a big slice of wedding cake. The driver had been pleased, but now it was evident that not even a very big slice of wedding cake with lemon custard filling was going to make up for the fact that his passengers were running very late.

Walking into the house, Heart called out, "Daed, Mary, the car and driver are waiting! It's time for you to go."

Her father replied immediately to her. "We're getting there, Heart. I'm just checking with Clayton about one last thing."

"Levi, I just told ya that I have your schedule handled. And I've talked to most everyone who recently commissioned work. They understand it's going to be a while."

"But—"

Clayton talked right over him. "In addition, you've already given me the phone number at the lake house. If there's a real problem that can't wait, I'll call you."

They were in the kitchen now, Levi and Mary and Clayton and Heart. Mary still looked radiant and lovely. Not bothered a bit by her new husband's tarrying.

Heart did not feel the same way. She tapped her foot.

Her father didn't notice. Instead, he drew out a scratch sheet of paper from one of his pockets and pulled on his reading glasses. "Now, Heart, about your—"

No way were they going to go over the same ten details yet again! Walking to his side, she gripped his arms and interrupted him. "Daed, I love you."

"I love you, too, Heart."

"You know that the farm is going to be fine, and I will be, too. Please stop worrying."

"But—"

Her voice gentled. "Clayton takes care of me, and I take care of everything else."

His mouth opened. Shut. At last, he nodded. "I suppose you have a point."

"I know I do."

Everything in her father's features softened. "Walk me out, wouldja?"

"Sure."

Obviously noticing that the two of them needed a minute, Mary said, "Clayton, how about you walk me to the car? I'll wait for Levi there."

"Sounds good."

"Goodbye, Heart," Mary said as she hugged her tightly. "I'll see you in two weeks."

"Yes, you will. Have a great time." As they hugged again, Heart noticed Clayton hugging her father.

"Don't wait too long," Mary warned her *daed*. "The driver will get cranky and so will I."

"I can't have that. Just give me a moment."

Seconds later, the door opened and shut, leaving Heart alone with her father.

"Are you ready now, Daed?" she asked gently.

"Almost." He reached for her hand.

Automatically Heart closed her fingertips around his. In spite of the fact that she was now happily married, Heart felt a warm, cozy feeling envelop her. Just as it always had since she was small.

After only three steps her father stopped again. Cleared his throat. "Ah, Heart, it occurred to me the other day that I never told you something about your name."

She smiled up at him, wondering why in the world he was thinking about such a thing. "My name? Do you mean Hazel?"

"*Nee.*" Very softly he continued, "I mean your *real* name. Heart."

"I . . . I don't understand."

Still holding her hand in his, he bent down slightly. Just a little bit. Just enough so she could look into his eyes. The blue eyes that she'd inherited from him.

"You see, your mother had her mind set on Hazel. She liked that name. A lot." He pursed his lips. "However, the truth was that I never was too excited about it."

She bit her lip to keep from smiling. "No?"

"No. But what could I do? Your mother hadn't had too easy a pregnancy and that's what she wanted to name our baby girl. It was easier to let her have her way, ain't so?"

She nodded.

"But then later, when you started fussing about your name and all . . . I couldn't help but think you might have had a point. Hazel never really did suit you."

She had a sudden lump in her throat. "But you thought Heart did."

Looking as if he also had a lump in his throat, he nodded. "You see . . . from the moment you appeared on God's green earth, I knew you had my heart." Releasing her fingers, he curved both of his hands around her face. "I've always loved you with everything I am, Heart. You made my life better and you've made my world brighter. I . . . I just thought you should know that."

Tears were falling down her cheeks. His eyes looked damp as well. She swallowed hard. "I think we'd best get you on your way, Daed."

Pressing a kiss to her cheek, he nodded. "I reckon you're right. See you in two weeks."

He turned, grabbed his straw hat, which had been carelessly tossed on the counter, and then strode out the back door.

Heart hurried out after him.

"You all right?" Clayton asked as they watched her father and Mary get situated, say something to the driver, and then turn and wave to them.

"*Jah*. I'm good," she whispered.

Clayton scanned her face, seemed to be satisfied with whatever he saw, and then raised his hand to wave goodbye to the happy couple.

She did the same and kept waving until they were out of sight.

And then they were gone.

"We did it," she proclaimed with a smile. "Daed and Mary are married at last."

"And gone!" Clayton added as he picked her up and twirled her in a circle. "Are you ready to go inside and collapse?"

"More than ready. I'm sure Spike is anxious to get out of his cage, too."

"Maybe so . . . but not as much as Virginia and Trouble," he teased as he led her inside. They kicked off their shoes right away and walked into the house in bare feet.

It was spring, the sun was shining, and both her father and she were happily married to spouses they truly loved. Living happily ever after.

It had been a perfect day. No, just another day in a perfect life. She was blessed.

Please read on for an excerpt from Shelley Shepard Gray's next Amish romance, *A IS FOR AMISH*.

He renews my strength. He guides me along the right paths, bringing honor to His name.
Psalm 23:3

A happy home is not merely having a roof over your head but having a foundation under your feet.
Amish proverb

Chapter 1

August

It had been a while since they'd all been in one car together. Since each of his siblings lived in different suburbs and hamlets around the Cleveland area, whenever the four of them did get together, it was easiest to simply meet at a restaurant for a quick bite to eat.

Today was different, though.

Even though Martin was the oldest boy and the one driving, he felt just as nervous as his younger brother Jonny. He held the steering wheel in a death grip and worst-case scenarios kept running through his head.

What in the world were they thinking about doing? Had they lost their ever-loving minds?

"You okay up there, Martin?" Kelsey asked.

"Yeah, why?"

"Oh, I don't know. Maybe because you've been wearing a permanent frown for the last ten miles."

Kelsey, all curly blond hair and blue eyes, was the closest to him in age. She was twenty-two to his twenty-three—except for two months during the year. Then they were the same age. Beth was the oldest at twenty-five and Jonny the youngest at twenty.

"Have I been frowning? I didn't realize it."

"You sure are," Jonny said. "And the reason I noticed is because I've been frowning just as much. Guys, I can't believe we're actually thinking about doing this."

Even though he'd been just thinking the very thing, Martin felt obligated to calm his brother's worries. "Remember, all we're doing is thinking about this. Don't forget, if we change our minds this afternoon, no one will even know. Especially not Mommi and Dawdi."

"They know something's up with us," Beth chimed in from the passenger seat next to him. "Mommi sounded pretty skeptical when I told her that the four of us want to pay them a visit because we haven't seen them in a while."

"Has it really been that long since any of us went to visit?" Kelsey asked.

"I saw them around Easter," Beth said. "None of you could make it." Just as it did when they were all in elementary school, her voice carried a hint of criticism.

Martin groaned. "Don't act like I blew you off. I

told you that I was stuck going to Cara's parents' house with her."

"I didn't say you blew me off, Martin." Her voice softened. "I am sorry that you two broke up."

"I thought she broke up with you, Martin," Jonny said.

She had. He hadn't tried to change her mind, though. He'd met Cara at work and had thought the snarky comments she made behind their customers' backs meant that she was fun. He'd soon found out that she was simply mean.

Pushing thoughts of Cara aside, Martin said, "I called our grandparents just last month. They were doing well."

"I'm not going to lie," Kelsey said. "I haven't seen either Mommi or Dawdi in almost a year. In fact, the last time Mommi called and left a message, I forgot to call her back."

"You had school. She understood."

"I know, but that's hardly an excuse. What about you, Jonny?"

"Um, well, I drove down to see them last month."

"You never told me that," Beth said.

"Why did you need to know?" His tone was a little defensive. Martin wondered why.

Beth didn't seem to notice, though. "Don't keep us in suspense. How were they?"

"The same as Mommi and Dawdi always are. They're good."

"You mean wonderful-*gut*," Kelsey teased.

Jonny chuckled. "Yeah. Anyway, we had a good time together. I drove them to a farmer's market in Berlin and then we cooked out in the backyard. It was awesome."

"Did you spend the night?"

"Yep. I wasn't planning on it, but I started thinking that I would rather be with my grandparents than with my three roommates."

"Your friends are crazy," Kelsey chided. "I can't think of anyone who would rather be with them in that gross apartment than with Mommi and Dawdi."

"It isn't that gross."

"It's not that clean."

He chuckled. "I can't argue with you there, but would you expect any different? All of us are working and going to school."

"And going out."

"That's true. But anyway, I can't deny that it was good to sleep at their house. The sheets smelled so good and Grandma made cornmeal cakes, eggs, and bacon."

Martin's mouth watered. "Did she serve hot maple syrup with the corncake?"

"So . . . you liked being there?" Beth asked.

"Of course." He cleared his throat. "It was as good as it always is. All I'm saying is that noone would have passed up a chance to stay at their house if they could help it."

"Except for Mom and Dad," Kelsey said.

Glad he was approaching a stop light, Martin groaned. "Kelsey, why did you bring them up?"

"How could I not? I mean, aren't you thinking about Mom and Dad—and wondering how each of them is going to react if we actually go through with this plan?"

"Actually?" Beth turned around to look at their sister. "I thought we were all on the same page. I thought we were all going to Baltic today to tell our grandparents that we want to be Amish. Just like them."

"I think we're thinking about it . . . but who even knows?" Kelsey asked.

"Kels is right," Jonny said. "Mommi and Dawdi might put the brakes on this idea before we even do anything besides talk about it."

"I hope not," Kelsey said. "I've always kind of wanted to be Amish. If I back out now, I think I'm going to regret it."

"It's one thing to think about becoming Amish, it's another to actually go ahead and start the process," Martin said.

"We all know that, Martin," Jonny said. "Don't act as if we don't."

"Sorry. I guess that did sound condescending. The truth is that I'm sort of freaking out."

"You should pull over the car," Beth said.

"Why? Are you afraid I can't drive you three while I'm freaking out?"

"Maybe we don't want to be stuck in the back seat while your head is obviously not on the road," Kelsey said.

"I'm fine."

"Actually, I was thinking more along the lines of

your pulling over so we can talk through this again," Beth said.

Jonny groaned. "All we've done is talk. We Zoomed together three different nights this past week. What else do we really have to say?"

Martin pulled off to the side in an empty parking lot. "Let's get out for a minute."

For once none of them argued or questioned. They just unbuckled their seatbelts and got out.

And then, there they were. Standing together.

It brought back so many memories. Of them all standing together before church on Sundays. Getting ready to ride the bus to school together.

Wondering when their mother was coming home.

They all had their father's and grandfather's dark blue eyes. Jonny and Beth had their father's lanky build, while Kelsey favored their mom, and he seemed to follow in their mom's brother's steps. He'd been a football player in college and had been huge.

Beth crossed her arms over her chest. "I think we should be honest with each other. Each of us should rate how serious we are about becoming Amish."

This was a classic Beth move. Making a pronouncement and expecting the three of them to go along and being shocked when they didn't follow her lead immediately.

When he noticed Kelsey and Jonny exchanging looks . . . and that Beth wasn't volunteering to go first, he sighed.

She noticed. "What?"

Martin bit back the worst of the snarky comments running through his head. "Beth, really? We're suddenly supposed to say how much we want to be Amish?"

"I think it's a perfectly good idea."

"Fine. You go first."

She looked away. "How about you?"

"No. It was your idea. Go."

Her eyes darted to Jonny and Kelsey. Without looking their way, Martin knew they were gazing at her with the same expression he was.

She sighed. "Fine. I'm sixty percent."

"That's it?" Jonny asked.

"Leaving everything is going to be really hard. I'm not a hundred percent sure I want to do it. And don't get mad—I'm just being honest."

Jonny lifted his chin. "I'm ninety."

Martin was floored. Jonny was not only the youngest sibling, he also led the most *English* life. "Kels?"

"I'm somewhere in between. I guess seventy-five percent? What about you, Martin?"

"I don't know for sure. It fluctuates. Some days, when everything is going fine, I don't want to be Amish at all. Other times, something will happen or I'll get overwhelmed . . . and I'll be almost a hundred percent."

"That's unhelpful."

"I know. I'm a mental mess right now. My brain feels scrambled."

Beth worried her bottom lip. "Maybe we should have waited to be sure of what we want to do before visiting Mommi and Dawdi."

"I wanted to see them," Kelsey said. "Didn't you?"

"Of course. I'm just saying . . ." Her voice drifted off. "I'm just trying to be honest here."

"There's nothing wrong with that," Martin said. "If we can't be honest with each other, then we're never going to be okay."

"That's what this is all about, anyway, right?" Jonny asked. "Don't we all just want to one day be okay?"

No one replied as they got back into the car, but no one needed to.

That statement, at least, had been something all of them could agree upon.

Visit our website at
KensingtonBooks.com
to sign up for our newsletters, read
more from your favorite authors, see
books by series, view reading group
guides, and more!

Become a Part of Our
Between the Chapters Book Club
Community and Join the Conversation